EBURY PRESS

NIGHT IN THE HILLS

Born in Baramulla, Kashmir, Manav Kaul has been an integral part of the film and theatre world, acting, directing and writing for the past twenty years. With each of his new plays, Manav has made people sit up and take notice, and he has created an equally valuable body of work as a writer. His books *Theek Tumhare Peechhe* (Right Behind You) and *Prem Kabootar* (Night in the Hills) have been dominating the Nielsen bestseller list.

Pooja Priyamvada is an author, columnist, professional translator, and content and language consultant. She is recognized as one of the '50 Powerful Women of 2022' by Fox Story India. She has also won several awards, including the India Prime Women Icon Award 2022 by Foxclues and the Shiksha Gaurav Puraskar 2023 by Universal Mentors Association and Brainwonders.

NIGHT IN THE HILLS

MANAV KAUL

Translated from the Hindi by
POOJA PRIYAMVADA

EBURY
PRESS

An imprint of Penguin Random House

EBURY PRESS

Ebury Press is an imprint of the Penguin Random House group of companies
whose addresses can be found at global.penguinrandomhouse.com

Published by Penguin Random House India Pvt. Ltd
4th Floor, Capital Tower 1, MG Road,
Gurugram 122 002, Haryana, India

First published as *Prem Kabootar* by Hind Yugm 2017
Published in Ebury Press by Penguin Random House India 2024

ISBN 9780143473961

Typeset in Adobe Caslon Pro by Manipal Technologies Limited, Manipal
Printed at Gopsons Papers Pvt. Ltd., Noida

www.penguin.co.in

MIX
Paper | Supporting
responsible forestry
FSC® C191020

Contents

I Have Moved on from This Realm a Long Time Ago . . .

I remember those windows and balconies of my childhood that opened into a wholly different world. I always had time to indulge in idleness of this world, full as it was of deep solitude. It made me feel like a farmer who, after a lot of hard work, waits . . . for the rain, for the seeds to burst open and for the crops to sway. However, I was not very fortunate. While I had sown some of myself in those deep solitudes, a lot of me has remained scattered all over the house. And when the scattering became too much to bear, making it difficult to move around in the house, I simply changed my home. These stories remind me of those countless homes! And in all those homes, I see that person who used to write. While he is still there, peeping through those very same windows and balconies, I have passed on and moved into a different realm. I am not him . . . not at all. I have simply endured him in different phases, from house to house. If one were to ask him about

1

me, I am sure he will have a similar opinion. To meet him is to surrender to him. For it is not possible to have any conversation without surrendering.

A lot of the scattered residue of my being that had gotten left behind has been safely preserved by him . . . the one who writes. It is because of the residue that I am excited to meet him repeatedly. Today, when people recognize me because of my writing, or ask questions, I experience a strange, other being answering on behalf of the writer. Because I am not the one who has written these stories. I have moved on long ago.

I returned to Baramulla after twenty-seven years. Khwazbagh, the colony where I was born and spent my childhood, was in ruins. I had to break open the door of my home to enter it. The house was like some time-worn, decaying person on his death bed, waiting for someone he could call his own before he would finally collapse. Suddenly, my gaze wandered to a little niche in one of the walls where I used to hide my toffees, and I couldn't control my emotions anymore.

Roaming around in the colony for hours, I went to all those lanes where I used to play. As I was about to leave, a woman asked: 'Who are you? What are you doing here?' I told her that I was born here; that I used to live in the last house in the lane. As soon as I had uttered the sentence, I realized how untrue, perhaps irrelevant, it was. The woman smiled; she didn't believe me. I walked away from there. At this moment, as I read my own stories, I experience the same feeling. I do feel the existence of each of my stories within me accompanied by a deep insight. Yet, as soon as I have said it, the feeling ceases to exist. Spoken words seem petty compared to existence.

I am an atheist. It is my stories that have kept me going in my trying times. I have survived because of my writing. This enormous banyan tree of words has sheltered me from harsh days in the sun. One could call it escapism, but the oddness of this world enchants me immensely. The not-so-heroic characters of my stories, too, enchant me. The drama that one witnesses in the world of losers is far more alluring to me than the charm of the winners. The satisfaction of bringing my stories to a conclusion—the pleasure of my losers arriving home—stays with me for a long time.

Though I have found love in my life, I have understood it only through my writing.

MANAV KAUL

A Bunch of Old Letters

Those were the days when I envied Salim. He would ask us to meet him each morning at the *maidan*, and I would drag Raju along. My afternoons were spent at Raju's tea shop. Salim was a tailor; but it always seemed like he was capable of doing much more. There was something about him. While Raju and I waited for Salim to arrive at the maidan, we would sit and chat. It now feels like a wonder that we had so much to talk about! And that each conversation was full of laughter that lasted until long after! We could talk for hours, Raju and me.

Salim would arrive with a football and make us both dance to his tune for hours. Despite repeated reminders, Raju would come to the maidan wearing his chappals. I wore my Goldstar shoes that had cost Rs 150. My father had bought them for me after much coaxing. I could not tolerate a single scratch on those shoes; that's the reason I could never play much football. Salim owned a pair of proper football shoes, the ones with studs on the outsole for a better grip. He had a small-built and had curly hair that he fashioned in a different style every few months. How I wished I had hair like his instead of the straight, broom-like mop that I was cursed with, which perpetually threatened to poke my eyes. I also felt disadvantaged because of my height.

After displaying his talent with the football, Salim would take us for tea. Raju's tea shop was in the market and so we would go to Madan's tea shop which was closer to the maidan. He never charged Salim for tea. Perhaps Salim had a credit account with him, or maybe he liked Salim as much as I liked him. I never saw Salim making any payment. While sipping on tea, Salim would hold court and both Raju and I would be mesmerized by his talk. After finishing his tea, he would take us for a walk towards the shrine. A group of girls would pass us on their bicycles. Presumably, they were on their way to school. Salim was infatuated with one of them. What followed felt like an adventure. I really enjoyed it.

Salim would ask us to wait near the wall of the shrine. Two of the girls from the group would emerge, and Salim would start walking on the road very purposefully. One of the girls would pedal faster, overtake the other girl and wait near the bulwark. The second girl would overtake Salim and then stop her bicycle on the side. For a brief while, both of them would murmur to each other. This would be followed by silence. Salim would look around, secretively, watching out for any passers-by. And then they would arrive at the pinnacle of love: the exchange of love letters. After this, Salim would return to us. Mounted on their

bicycles, both the girls would disappear into the grove of
banyans and peepals.

I, too, was infatuated with the girl Salim liked. Not
just infatuated, I even began dreaming about her. I would
talk to her for hours in my dreams, though I didn't know
why I liked her so much. Perhaps it because she was
Salim's, and I liked Salim very much. I don't know. The
other girl would give me glances, but Raju believed she
was eyeing him. We were indecisive about who she was
interested in.

Our next task would be to hear Salim read out the love
letter. He would stand on the bulwark, while we stood by
it, and Salim would read the letter aloud.

Salim
You must be fine. I, too, am fine.

Listen . . . please don't stop by my house. My
brother suspects something and has already enquired
twice about you. Don't wear that orange shirt. You look
like a goon. Why don't you wear that red one? It looks
so nice! Gattu dared to stop me yesterday and asked me
to be friends with him. I told him, 'Have you looked
at yourself in the mirror?!' He is always following me.
When we meet next, wear the red shirt.

Everything else is fine. My friend likes your friend.
She wants to give him a letter. I told her that I would
first ask you. Tell me . . . should she give him a letter?

I'll write later.
Minakshi

Raju sported a thick moustache, and he coloured his hair with henna. He was taller than both Salim and me, and because he regularly went to the local gym, he had a tough body. Listening to Salim read the love letter, his mouth would turn agape, and his eyes would shine with incredulity. He couldn't believe that a girl could ever write him a love letter. He had assumed that such things could only happen in films or with Salim since he was the most experienced when it came to matters of the heart. Salim had even exchanged love letters with a teacher in the school in which Minakshi studied.

Both Raju and I were very excited. Whom did Minakshi's friend want to give the letter to? I didn't like the way Raju had looked at me: defeat was writ large in his eyes. Those were times when there were a number of films on friendship. We would all look for reasons to sacrifice ourselves for friendship. I had found a reason. I told Raju, 'I don't like that girl.'

'Then why do you give her glances as she passes by? Had you stayed hidden, this problem would not have occurred. By now, she would have given me the letter.' Raju said this laughingly, but I recognized the pain in those words. He was older than both of us. Salim resolved this issue. He said, 'Before the girl chooses, you choose.' Neither Raju nor I understood what he meant. Salim was suggesting that Raju must initiate things; that he must give the girl a letter. Salim also immediately decided that it should be done the very next day. Raju was to give that girl a love letter the following day. Raju's anxiety was apparent to me.

He was baffled. He said, 'Listen, I need to open the shop early today; I'll go now. We shall meet in the morning at the ground.' He ran away. Salim and I looked at each other and laughed.

While the idea of sacrificing for friendship was noble on its own, yet I don't know why I kept experiencing a strange jealousy all day. I had thought about writing a love letter for many days, and I began it with *Dear Minakshi* every time. Salim was the expert in matters of the heart. Both Raju and I were in the same boat. I suddenly started to feel that tomorrow Raju would be in Salim's boat, and I would remain lonely forever. A strange fear started to manifest inside of me. I began to feel as if someone was writing history; that some man was recording these small, meaningless things. Many years later, it would be said: Salim was first; Raju was second; and Sunil, who got the chance, but, in his silly attempt to sacrifice for friendship, in the spirit of films, stood third. Now he is lonely and will be third forever. I contemplated handing over a love letter to the second girl the following morning before these two arrived and before those girls reached the shrine. But I wanted to give that love letter to Minakshi.

Father was sitting in the outer room and was immersed in his journalism work. I quietly picked a blank sheet of paper from his table. As I reached my room, I heard a voice say, 'You are hardly at an age to make paper planes. How about studying instead?'

Father's journalistic career moved at the same pace as everything else did in the village: Raju's tea shop, Salim's tailoring business . . . Father blamed my mother for it: 'I was to go to Delhi; I stayed back because of that unfortunate one.'

My mother had passed away years ago. Father says Mother's illness had consumed his future. I remember Mother as a faint, pleasant memory, gradually turning into a black-and-white photograph on the wall. Once a year, it would be decorated with a garland of fresh flowers. To get rid of the hassle of getting a fresh garland every year, Father once bought a plastic garland and placed it on the photograph permanently. Since then, I have wanted to buy a new garland of fresh flowers and throw away this plastic one. But that day has kept getting postponed. Moreover, now the plastic garland seems all right to me, too.

I could not bring myself to write the name 'Minakshi' on the sheet of paper. So, I thought of her, placed her image in my heart and began writing my letter.

Dear ('Minakshi' in my heart),
I like bicycles. I have asked my father many times to buy me one, but he always postpones it to the next year. You ride yours well. I do not know how to ride a bicycle. One day, I helped Pappu fix the chain on his cycle. My hands became black with grease, but I learnt how to put a chain on a cycle. I sometimes accompany Pappu to get air filled in the tyres of his cycle. He makes me ride pillion, but I like to sit in the front. I did that with Rathore Uncle long ago. When a cycle moves over small pebbles, I like the crunching sound it makes. I will learn how to ride a cycle. I had once started riding along with Pappu, but he doesn't give me his cycle. If you accept

my friendship, I can learn to ride on your cycle. A ladies'
cycle is easier to learn on, says Pappu.

Rest is fine.

I didn't write my name at the end of the letter. I folded
the sheet and kept it safely in my pocket. I was scared
that I had named Pappu and Rathore Uncle in it, and
that could get me caught. But I was sure that I would
never garner enough courage to hand over this letter to
Minakshi anyway.

The next morning at the ground, Raju was rather quiet.
For the first time, we were both waiting for Salim without
saying a word to each other. I knew there was a love letter
in his pocket; his first love letter. My first love letter was in
my pocket, too. The person recording our history could not
as yet shunt me into the third place.

'Hey, Raju! All well?' I asked.

'Yes.'

'So, what is going on?' I asked again.

'What can go on?'

Silence. For the first time, Raju wasn't a friend. He
was waiting for Salim to say what he wanted to say. He
was sitting at a slight distance from me. I don't know why
but this seemed intolerable to me. I started running in the
maidan. When Salim arrived, Raju even refused to play
football. Salim and I played for some time, and then it
was time to go towards the shrine. Raju was only talking
to Salim.

'Salim, I couldn't write it.'

'What?'

'The letter.'

'Oh, dear! You should've written something.'

'I couldn't.'

'So, what will we do now?' Salim expressed concern and looked at me.

Raju was older than us. But at this moment, his situation evoked immense pity. I regretted having watched so many films on friendship and getting trapped in filmy nonsense. But all said and done, this was a golden opportunity to sacrifice myself for my friend. So, I took out the letter from my pocket and handed it to Salim.

'What's this?'

'A letter.'

'So, we have competition, eh champ?'

'No. I knew Raju wouldn't be able to write, so I wrote it for him.'

Sacrifice. True friendship. Renunciation. I was experiencing many emotions. My eyes welled up and Raju embraced me. We reached the bulwark and read the letter.

'Who is this Pappu?' Salim asked after hurriedly going through the letter.

'Pappu lives in my locality.'

'Okay.'

As Raju wrote his name at the end of the letter, Salim asked me, 'You really wrote this for Raju?' I nodded.

'What's the name of the girl?' Raju asked. None of us knew the girl's name, so it was decided that Raju would carry a pen, talk to her about friendship, and if she said 'yes', he would write her name on the letter and give it to her.

The girls came riding their cycles. This time, looking at Minakshi, I felt a strange ache. Only I knew that I had written that letter for Minakshi. The other girl went ahead and stopped at a distance, as usual. I was hiding behind the wall, as usual. However, what was different this time was that both Raju and Salim went ahead, and both had a letter each in their pockets. The person recording the history of our friendship was probably laughing.

On the podium where winners stand to receive their trophies, I stood third and a sad song played in the background.

Raju was very scared. He was walking towards the girl. The moment he reached her . . . I couldn't bear to witness this meeting any longer and began running home. Friendship could go take a walk! To hell with the promises of friendship! All the melodrama in the films . . . it was all untrue! I felt like a fool; like someone who first inflicts wounds upon himself, and then rubs salt on those very wounds! Enough . . . enough . . . enough. Salim was welcome to form opinions about me. Raju and his moustache could go to hell. I kept running . . .

Afternoons can be strange sometimes. This afternoon, today, doesn't seem like a part of my life. I am frantically pacing between the kitchen and the outer room. Father is at his desk, scribbling on sheets of paper as usual. Suddenly, he says, 'We always feel attracted to someone who is beyond our reach; once they are within our reach, the attraction gets diluted like water in milk.' I stare at Father in utter disbelief. After a while, I leave the house. The thought of Raju giving the letter to the girl persistently occupies my mind space. What might have transpired between them? Would she have liked Raju? Would Minakshi also begin to like Raju? With a start, I realized that my thoughts and I had arrived at Raju's tea shop.

Salim was noisily gulping down tea, and Raju appeared happy. A miracle had taken place for the first time in his life. The girl had promised to give him a letter as well. Meanwhile, I was wondering why I wasn't feeling happy. Salim mentioned that Minakshi had not given him a letter. She had, for the first time, brought up the fact that Salim was a Muslim. Somehow, this had amused Salim, and he was laughing a lot. I, too, started to laugh and Raju said that she wasn't wrong in bringing it up. 'She is a *Pandit*, and you are a *Muslim*,' Raju said. He added that it wasn't right. Somehow, amongst the three of us, this topic had never come up in our conversations. Salim and I continued to laugh, and the matter ended there.

Something was changing within me. I was spending more time in my room and enjoying reading stories. *Dharamyug*, a Hindi magazine, used to be delivered to our house regularly, and the stories and poems it contained interested me. Each story, when I read it, seemed like it was set in my village. I even knew all the characters. When I spoke about this to Raju and Salim, they listened quietly and kept looking at me. Perhaps that was the only time when they quietly listened to me. I would, on purpose, narrate to them stories of foreign writers. They were in awe of Vladimir Mayakovsky. A strange satisfaction would overcome me; it was sweet revenge. As much over Raju and Salim as over the one who was recording the history of insignificant things;

the one who had placed me third. Here was one place where I stood first—this world of literature, and of stories that communicated with me. While I stood first, Raju and Salim could fight for the second and third position. What did I care—it was their matter!

One day, Raju came running to my home. 'Who's this Pappu?' Raju asked point-blank. 'Pappu? Raju, what are you talking about?'

'I am asking you, and you are questioning me?'

'What are you asking?'

'Who's this Pappu, the one you mentioned in the letter?'

'Oh, him . . . no one in particular; he lives in my colony.'

'What was the need to mention him?'

'How do I know? . . . I was simply trying to help you.'

Raju was sweating profusely as he held a letter in his hand. He took out a white handkerchief from his pocket; it was sprinkled with talcum powder. He wiped his whole face with the handkerchief and handed me that letter.

I read the letter.

I made Minakshi read your letter. I hope you don't mind that? She is my dearest friend; she makes me read all of Salim's letters. We never hide anything from each other. Your letter is very different from the way you talk. It's good. Minakshi also liked the letter. Why doesn't Pappu let you ride his cycle? Is Pappu your friend? When he takes you along to get air filled in the tyres, why don't you ride the cycle then? Make him sit pillion. I don't give my cycle to anyone, not even to my sister. If you go towards the river in the evening, let me know. I go there every day at 6 p.m. to pray at the Kale Mahadev, but it is very crowded there. Keep your distance from me.

Why don't you wear a belt with your trousers?

Neena

Raju was now wearing a belt. People act absurdly in the game of love, says my father. I was very happy that Minakshi had liked the letter. I asked Raju for some time to write a letter in response. I again picked up a blank sheet of paper from Father's table. I told Raju to go and assured him that I would give him the letter in the evening.

'Oh! But why not write it now and give it to me right away?'

'No, I can't write when someone is watching. I can only write when I am alone.'

'Okay. And listen, write good things about me in the letter.'

'But it's not I who is writing the letter; it's you. How will you praise your own self in the letter?'

'Oh, yes! But write a good letter.'

'I will try.'

'Bring it to the shop in the evening. I am going now.'

Raju walked away. Making use of this time of the day—when Father was usually at the village square, where discussions about changing the world take place over rounds of tea and paan—I decided to write the love letter. I picked up the page I had taken from Father's table, and thinking of Minakshi, taking her name many times, I began to write. Love truly turns one into a cuckoo. But who was the cuckoo: Raju or I? Uff! Write . . . write . . . write . . . words were evading me. I wrote something and then tore it up. I wrote again, and again I tore it up. What should I write? What should I say about Pappu? After I tore up a few sheets of paper, a story occurred to me. Like a talisman, I repeated her name and started to write.

I asked Pappu if I could borrow his cycle. It is then that he told me he loves a girl and loves her deeply. The kind of love that makes a person go crazy. Out of sheer love, he used to lend her his cycle when she would go for her tuitions. After a long time, he came to know that, before going to her tuitions, she would go and meet a boy in Professors' Colony. You might wonder how Pappu came to know of this. It so happened that, one day, by chance, Pappu found a love letter from that boy addressed to that girl. Since that day he never lends his cycle to anyone. He lets me ride pillion only because I am his friend, otherwise he doesn't even allow that.

I liked reading your letter. I have no issues if you let Minakshi read my letters. I will come to Kale Mahadev today to see you, to watch you from a distance. Come to my shop sometime to have tea.

I shall write more in the next letter.

Raju

Raju came by in the evening, hurriedly took the letter, and left. He had to go to Kale Mahadev. I noticed that his style of walking had changed, and he was now strutting about. I was again reminded of what my father said. Clearly, Raju was going crazy.

This is what is called fiction . . . these imaginary stories; the ones that are a creation of the mind and are not true in real life. I had written an imaginary story about Pappu. He had never lent me his cycle because he hardly knew me. I would have assumed that no one would be interested in the tale of a rejected lover. I was wrong! Most stories that do become well-known are the ones about dejected lovers. Uff!

An exasperated Raju came to see me after two days.

'Oh, boy! What is this nonsense that you have created?'

I read the reply that girl had sent. Her letter contained only two sentences: '*Poor Pappu! Who is that girl? What happened next?*'

'I had asked you to put an end to the Pappu episode. You've made him larger than life!'

'I did end Pappu's story. What was I to do! Henceforth, I will not even mention Pappu. Give me her letter; I will write a reply.'

'We are stuck now. While handing over her letter, she told me she wanted to know everything about Pappu!'

'And what about Minakshi?'

'She went a step further; she asked me the name of the girl.'

'Which girl?'

'Damn! Pappu's girl; the one who made a fool out of him.'

I could write; I could write randomly—but Pappu . . . I didn't know much about Pappu. And that girl . . . Minakshi was curious about the girl? I liked that. But who was she? Forget her, who was Pappu? Well, in the storytelling domain, it was I who held the first position. So, I took this as a challenge.

Raju was still standing there. He took out a slip of paper from his pocket. Handing it to me, he said, 'This is a list of the ten benefits of tea. Write this in the reply. Get Neena interested in tea.'

Completely sidelining Pappu in the reply, I only talked about tea. Citing some ten benefits of tea, I urged Neena to come to the market square. Raju was proud of his tea-making skills, but I doubted whether they could impress a girl. Yet, I toed the line and did what Raju asked me to do. I had read about writers: that they think deeply, and never let anyone interfere with their writing. I had allowed Raju to butt in and wasn't feeling good about it. My fear came true; the reply was bad. Neena was not a tea drinker. She even went on to say that if Raju was going to write similar letters in the future, he need not bother writing any more. Raju's first love was about to become his last. Near the ruins of the old fort was a dense peepal tree; our regular haunt. I had already narrated to Salim the entire episode. Raju arrived at the spot after a while.

'Listen, you continue writing about Pappu. What a nuisance this is!' said an irritated Raju.

'Oh! You seem to be fed up right at the onset of love!' said Salim.

'I feel like a postman. This Sunil is narrating Pappu's tale to Neena, and I am like a foolish monkey in between!'

'By the way, Sunil, who is this Pappu? Minakshi was telling me about some girl who made a fool out of him. What is all this nonsense?' Salim asked me.

I felt they were critics, pointing fingers at me as a writer. At least in front of these two, I was very serious about my writing. I began the conversation at a deeper level.

'I will now need to know everything about Pappu. Research! What he does, whom does he meet, etc., etc.'

'Why?' asked Raju.

'In order to bring an end to Pappu's tale, we need to know everything about him. Writing a false story is like cheating your own self,' I said.

Raju and Salim were astonished to hear me.

There was silence for some time, and then Salim said, 'Listen, brother, whatever it is . . . just bring an end to it and set up Raju properly with the girl.'

'Yes, my friend, it is as simple as that,' Raju emphasized.

I chose to remain silent because the matter was beyond my comprehension. I didn't know how to turn the situation around.

In the evening, I found myself in front of Mishra Tent House. There was a huge signboard in front of the house. I called out: 'Pappu Bhai, Pappu Bhai!'

Pappu emerged from the house in his vest. It was a size smaller than he required and was ill-fitting on his frail form. His odd-looking navel was visible. Pappu must have been around twenty-seven years old. His tent business was doing well. Financially, he was the most successful amongst us.

'Yes, Sunil, tell me . . . what brings you here?'

'I needed to borrow your cycle.'

'Cycle?'

'Yes, you had an Atlas Goldline, didn't you?'

'Oh! It is punctured and is parked in the backyard. I bought a Bajaj Chetak. But I keep it near the store. Here, in the front yard, the neighbours cast their evil eye on it.'

'I hadn't seen the cycle for many days, so I thought . . .'

There was silence after that. I didn't know how to carry forward the conversation. There was hair around his navel, his teeth were yellowing, and his legs were lanky. How could I fabricate a story about him!

I asked him abruptly, 'So . . . the negotiations for your marriage must be on! Whom do you intend to marry?'

My tone was teasing. Pappu was older than me, and we were not even friends. Suddenly, his facial muscles tightened.

'So, you have come to make fun of me? You scoundrel, you came here to make fun of me!'

'No, Pappu Bhai . . . I just . . . I shall go.'

I ran away from there.

At times, I wonder about how we hoard our dreams. When we observe a friend experiencing happiness in the company of someone, we presume that it will be the same for us some day; that we, too, shall feel happy with a companion. This dream of everlasting happiness also creates a chasm deep within our being. And until the chasm exists, until that gap between dream and reality is bridged, it nags us. The beloved's image arouses a feeling of intense longing. And only the beloved can douse the fire of that longing and fill the chasm between dream and reality. We see other people's lives and their images keep getting registered somewhere in an empty space within us. We gradually take out these images and try and match them with our lives. We wonder if we have lived in the same way as those other people. My dreams were full of Minakshi. I aspired to be able to give her just one letter that began 'Dear Minakshi'. I wrote many such letters but was never able to give them to her. Her name was scribbled all over in the empty space within me.

I felt like meeting Salim. He always had a solution for everything. When I crossed the market square, Father was standing near the paan cart talking to Lohiaji. He always called out to me in people's presence; he needed to assert his control over me.

'Oye, come here, oye!'

I first pretended not to hear him, and then I said, 'Oh! Father, you! Here?'

The entire village is aware that Father can be found in the market square at this hour every single day. Yet, whenever I come across him in the market, I have to act surprised at finding him there because he never agrees to the fact. 'Yes, I came this side. Okay, tell me, how is the name Sonakshi?'

'Good,' I said.

'Okay.'

He took out a diary from his pocket and wrote the name Sonakshi in it. He didn't need me any longer. Walking away from him I realized . . . the name Sonakshi was similar to Minakshi.

I was sitting in Salim's shop. His father had Nepalese features. Salim's younger brother was working in the rear part of the shop, marking a fabric in blue, to be stitched as a shirt. Salim, who was in the front part of the shop, was cutting another fabric, for a pair of pants. We remained quiet in his father's presence. Salim's hands worked like magic on fabric. In the time that his father stitched one pair of pants, Salim was able to do three. His work responsibility was stitching two pairs of pants and one shirt every day. As long as he did that, he was free to spend the rest of the day as he liked. No one asked him any questions. I filed away another image: of two pairs of pants and a shirt. As I was comparing this image with the emptiness of my life, I heard Salim say, 'Let's go,' and my dream was shattered. We walked straight towards the fort. As soon as we sat under the peepal tree, Salim asked: 'What did you find out about Pappu?'

'He is a very shy guy and doesn't step out of his home much. He usually sits in the backyard of his house. He barely spoke to me.'

'And who is the girl who cheated him?'

'Her name is Sonakshi. She is very beautiful.'

'Have you seen her?'

'Yes, she is amazing. Prettier even than your Minakshi.'

'Where does she live?'

'She is from Peru village. At times, Pappu goes all the way to the village on his cycle simply to get a glimpse of her. He was saying that someday he might take me along.'

'Peru village is so far away. Pappu goes there on his cycle?'

'Oh, yes, Salim! What to do! Love turns one into a cuckoo . . .'

My story was beginning to take shape as I was talking to Salim. Though I was fabricating lies to impress Salim, it was in Pappu's Sonakshi that I had found my Minakshi. It was surprising how I had impulsively named Pappu's girl 'Sonakshi'.

When I asked Salim about Minakshi, he said, 'She comes from a very rich family. Her father is a doctor. He owns Prabhat Nursing Home.'

'Do you love her?' Why did I ask him that? The word 'love' did not go too well with Salim.

'I love her as much as she loves me. I have asked her to meet me at Nehru Park at 3 p.m. tomorrow. It'll be fun if she does come.'

'In Nehru Park?'

'Yes, it's deserted at that hour. I have told her to come to the bench behind the kids' swings. Don't tell anyone.'

Jealousy is not a word; it is a feeling that courses through one's being like salt rubbed on wounds. I didn't want Minakshi to meet Salim in the park. Soon as I felt I couldn't breathe. I told Salim that I had to go home.

'Oye, Raju is about to come. Wait for a bit!' 'No, I will meet you tomorrow morning at the ground.'

I didn't go to the ground the following day. Instead, I sulked at home. Father was busy with his

English tuitions in the outer room. There were only two rooms in the house: the kitchen, and the outer room. For the duration of the tuitions, I preferred to stay in the kitchen. If I hung about outside, Father would often entrap me as well in his English. So, using my homework as an excuse, I remained seated inside the kitchen. The hands of the clock were quickly turning from one to two. Minakshi must have started for Nehru Park. How would she reach? What would they do in Nehru Park? I was pacing in the kitchen. Father called from outside: 'Oye, make me a cup of tea.'

I put the kettle to boil. My restlessness was growing with the boiling tea. I have a few bad habits. One of them is that sometimes things grow inside me, so much so that they become larger than life. I could, in that moment, see Minakshi entering Nehru Park . . . meeting Salim, and . . . the tea spilled over. Father scolded me. I even dropped the cup. It didn't break because it was a steel cup, but the noise it made compelled Father to come to the kitchen.

'Why, birdie, where are you flying off to?'

Each time my father was furious at me, he would call me a bird. Flying is equivalent to escaping. He was right! Why should a human being fly; only birds must fly! I was flying uselessly like a vulture over Nehru Park. I was speechless in front of my father. I experienced this often. When I couldn't understand something, I went numb. I believed that even a slight movement on my part would ruin the situation further. So even if all hell were to break loose, I would not budge from my place.

'Stupid! Look, it is spilling over again. Switch off the gas. Switch it off. You fool, switch it off!'

Giving me a tight slap, Father switched off the gas stove himself. The children sitting outside started to laugh. I wore my slippers and went out of the house.

Father would hit me every now and then over petty things. It felt strange. I was grown up. His slap was never wasted though; each time Father slapped me, someone or the other was around to laugh at me. I wish my black-and-white mother were around. Someone—anyone—to whom I could complain against my father.

I was in front of Nehru Park. It was almost 3 p.m. by my watch. I rushed into the park and went straight towards the kids' swings and hid behind the mango tree. Suddenly, I was filled with a strong and intense longing. It felt as if someone had shot me in the chest. I saw Minakshi approaching; she was wearing a yellow salwar-kameez, white dupatta and red sandals. I was seeing her without her cycle for the first time. She was so beautiful. So beautiful! Then I saw Salim walking behind her. Spotting Minakshi, Salim turned towards the other side to check. Minakshi went and sat on the bench. Her back was towards me. She wasn't looking at Salim. She was playing with her white dupatta. How I wished

I could go and sit beside her! I had so much to tell her: the stories of my father's beatings, my black-and-white mother, also Pappu's story and my desire to give her a love letter . . .

Just then, Salim came and sat beside her. I could not hear what they were saying. In some time, Salim edged closer. He was laughing and held Minakshi's hand. I began to cry. I didn't know why I felt like crying. I didn't want to cry. I just wanted to go away from there; yet I remained rooted. Then, all of a sudden, I uttered Minakshi's name! She turned around to look at me; her gaze met mine and I stood shocked. I couldn't move at all. I wanted to hide behind the tree, but my feet had turned to stone. My eyes froze. She turned away and started to look at Salim again, ignoring me completely. As soon as I had recovered enough, I attempted to run away from there but tripped. I didn't have the courage to look back. I didn't know if Salim had seen me or not. I pulled myself up and began to run.

I didn't want to go home. I went straight to Raju's tea shop. He was happy to see me, and immediately offered me a cup of strong chai. There weren't many customers at his shop. He asked, 'What happened? Why didn't you come in the morning?'

'I didn't wake up early enough.'

I wondered why I had begun to lie so much! What's more, I even had a convincing story to go along with every lie. Suddenly, my eyes welled up. It wasn't about Minakshi; I didn't know what it was. I began to cry. Raju got worried.

'What happened? Is everything all right? Did your father hit you again? Oh! Why don't you speak up?'

I stepped out of the shop to wash my face at the tap. Had I not done that, I might have blurted out the truth to Raju. At the tap, I had some time to think, and yet another false story was born inside me. My story.

I went back. Raju was waiting.

'I just met Pappu.'

'So?'

'When I reached Pappu's home, his father told me Pappu was in the backyard and had not been talking to anyone since the morning.'

Something triggered inside me and as I was talking to Raju, Pappu's father seemed like my father—only better groomed, weak, pitiable, a clerk in some government office, wearing thick glasses and a safari suit. Did I really want a father like that? Perhaps the reason I enjoyed creating stories so much was because I could find in the imaginary world what I couldn't have in real life.

I returned to my story.

'Pappu's father is a clerk in the municipality. I went to the backyard. Pappu was indeed sitting there, wearing a white shirt. With his mop of curly hair, he was sitting in a big chair holding a thick book. The moment I went closer to him he said, "Leave me alone. I don't want to speak to anyone." I asked Pappu what had happened. He remained silent for a while and then said he had cycled to Peru village in the morning. He had wanted to see Sonakshi after many days. The moment he reached Peru, he saw Sonakshi entering Gandhi Park. He quietly followed her, and parking the cycle aside, he, too, entered the park and hid behind a mango tree. Sonakshi was sitting on a bench with her back towards him; no . . . not her back, but her face towards him.'

'What are you saying?' Raju said with a hint of irritation.

'I am trying to remember what Pappu told me.'

'Oh! Why don't you simply tell me what happened in the end?'

'It doesn't work like that; you have to listen to the whole story. The poor fellow has suffered so much and all you want to know is what happened in the end.'

'Okay, so why are you getting so angry? Tell me the story.'

'This village doesn't care a dime about tragedy!'

'Wait . . . let me serve tea to my customers.'

'Are you going to serve tea now?'

'Yeah! There are customers; let me serve them tea and then come back to listen to the story. Pappu isn't dead yet anyway.'

I couldn't control my anger.

'You listen! I am not writing any more letters for you. Go and do whatever you want to!'

'To hell with the letter! Why are you shouting? I can meet her without a letter anyway.'

I left Raju's shop. If I went home, Father would be sitting at his desk filing away all the rotten news that he would have gathered from the village: a two-headed snake was found in so-and-so's field; a goat was feeding a piglet; ants were seen crawling out of a man's ear . . . My father had to make all these snippets of so-called news interesting. And I was at the receiving end of his frustration. So, I decided not to go home. Instead, I went to the riverbank . . . for peace, and for some solitude. I was looking for quietude for the first time. I knew that writers did this. Yes, accomplished writers. But why me?

Humidity hung heavy in the air. A strong wind was blowing. The waters of the river seemed turbulent. I sat huddled on a rostrum, in the shade. I only had two friends, Salim and Raju, and I was hiding from them. What had happened to me? I was not such a person. The plan was to write a simple love letter and hand it to Raju. But then I had extended the story. I could still have ended it there, but I didn't. Both Salim and Raju now knew about Sonakshi. I would have to cook up a story in a way that neither of them suspected anything. Arriving at this conclusion, I felt at peace with myself. I lay down on the rostrum and began to think about the contents of the love letter that I would give to Raju. I wondered what would happen next.

So, Minakshi . . . no, not Minakshi, it was Sonakshi . . . was sitting on a bench in Gandhi Park, facing Pappu. For a long time, she kept playing with her dupatta. Suddenly, Pappu decides not to hide behind the tree anymore. Sonakshi sees him but pretends not to. Pappu is about to walk towards her but right then he spots that boy from the Professors' Colony. Pappu hides behind the tree again. The boy comes and engages Sonakshi in conversation. (I name the boy Raju in the story; there is a Raju at every crossroad in this country, and I am also taking revenge on Raju in this manner.) Sonakshi is sitting quietly. She then covers Raju's mouth with her hand and stops him from talking. She pulls him closer in an embrace. While embracing Raju, she is facing Pappu and looking at him. Pappu should have left then, but he didn't. She embraced the boy from the Professors' Colony many times. Pappu didn't leave; he stood there crying.

When I opened my eyes, I realized I had fallen asleep on the rostrum. It felt like my imagined story was a reality; that it had actually happened. I got up and rushed home to write Raju's love letter before I forgot the plot.

The following morning, I reached the ground quite early. Raju came after a while. I didn't give him the letter. I wanted him to ask for it. We both remained silent. Then Salim arrived. He had neither brought the football nor was he wearing his football shoes. He had come to the ground wearing chappals for the first time. He walked straight up to me and kept staring at me for a long time. Before I could understand anything, he slapped me hard. Raju didn't understand anything either. He started shouting: 'What happened, friends, what happened?' But we both remained silent. Only Salim and I knew what that slap was for. I took out the letter from my pocket, gave it to Raju and quietly walked away from there.

'Raju and Salim were my best friends.' I wrote this sentence in my diary and kept staring at the word 'were' for a long time.

* * *

Many days had passed. Neither did I meet either of them nor did they try to get in touch. I was restless; I could not absorb myself in my mundane routine. How difficult it was to live with your own self: I wrote this sentence somewhere. I went out with utmost care, avoiding meeting either Raju or Salim. They were both a significant part of my life. I wondered how I was to spend my whole day. I began to meet Pappu Bhai a lot during this time. The imaginary story had ended. I had accepted the real Pappu. One day, Pappu made me sit pillion on his Bajaj Chetak and we went towards the bridge. When we reached the bridge, he took out a Wills cigarette. Since it was kept in his pocket, along with a matchbox, the cigarette was slightly bent. I was astonished. 'Pappu Bhai, do you smoke?' I asked.

'No, but I light one sometimes when I come here.' I found this very romantic. But all the romance vanished into thin air when the cigarette didn't light up as the wind was too strong. Behind the scooter, behind my back, Pappu even made me remove my shirt to create a cover, but it still didn't light up. I started laughing. He got so upset that he took his scooter and went to a shop on the other side of the bridge, lit the cigarette, came back and handed it to me. I held Pappu's cigarette like an incense stick and sat behind him on the scooter. Riding it fast and applying brakes right in the middle of the bridge, he parked it there. He sat on the seat, rested his feet on the ledge of the bridge, and asked for the cigarette. It was already half burnt-out, but Pappu Bhai wasn't bothered. He took a long drag, closed his eyes, and exhaled the smoke. The wind was playing with Pappu's hair. His eyes were closed, and he was exhaling smoke. I began to realize the shortcomings of the Pappu of my imaginary world. I felt that the Pappu of my story should also smoke. For the cigarette-like love-of-his-life—Sonakshi—he should annihilate himself. I suddenly began to long for Minakshi. It seemed like I had known her for ages, and we had been talking to each other a lot. She had been the subject of my dreams. She . . . now I, too, wanted to smoke a cigarette, but I immediately killed my wish.

'Oye, why did you talk about my marriage?'

'Just like that, Bhai! You are so awesome, so I thought . . . surely you are the one who must have kept the marriage on hold . . . otherwise . . . by now. . .'

'By now . . . what?'

It suddenly struck me that Pappu had brought me to this isolated place so that he could beat me up over the talk of marriage that I had initiated earlier.

'You are right; it would have happened by now. But the one I wanted to marry . . . I supplied all the tent material at her wedding.'

'Who was that girl?'

'You are having fun at my expense, aren't you?'

'Not at all, Pappu Bhai. You mentioned, so I asked.'

'She is married to someone in Peru village. Come, let's go to Peru today.'

After Pappu finished the cigarette, we left for Peru village on his scooter. I began to wonder about the interplay between reality and imagination—where one begins and the other ends, and how. It is such a thin line. Good that Pappu Bhai didn't name the girl. If the name were Sonakshi, I would probably have jumped from the bridge and committed suicide. We stopped in front of a house in Peru village. In the courtyard of the house was a huge peepal tree, and the nameplate on the big gate read 'D.M. Tiwari'. Pappu remained standing there for some time. To keep himself occupied, and perhaps to seem busy, he ordered tea from the shop across the house. Just then, the big gate of the Tiwaris opened and a white car came out. Pappu turned his face the other way. I managed to look inside the car, which was full of women. One amongst them was looking towards Pappu Bhai's scooter. Even after the car had gone past us, she turned back and kept looking at the scooter. Pappu Bhai kept his face turned towards the other side, his hair still catching the wind, and eyes restless.

I murmured her name: Sonakshi! In a few moments, the car had vanished from our sight.

To use my father's language: every person goes crazy. You talk to anyone; beneath the tough exterior shell, everyone goes crazy, especially when it comes to love. We rode back to our village on the scooter. Neither of us talked about the girl. Pappu Bhai dropped me home, and without saying anything, left for his own home. I was curious to know what was going through his mind. His silence could write an entire tragedy right away. On the other hand, the absolute silence between Raju, Salim and I was making me author a tragedy as well.

The simple act of ghost-writing a love letter for Raju had created Pappu's character, thus turning me into an author. I had begun to enjoy reading people's faces. Just as I didn't want to know the real name of Pappu's beloved, similarly, I had no interest in knowing people's real-life stories. I would watch their faces, their clothes, how they walked, and I felt a story was waiting to be created. However, as a writer, I made a mistake. I began to document my stories in a diary, including Pappu's story. I don't know when my father found the secret place, I used to hide it in. He had probably been reading it for a while. As time passed, I tried to make new friends. But they were nothing like Salim and Raju. These new friends would get bored listening to my stories.

One fine morning, I went to the ground. Salim and Raju were playing football as usual. As soon as they saw me, they stopped playing. We kept looking at each other for some time but no one said anything. Salim gestured to Raju, and they began to walk towards the fort. I also turned around and began to walk towards my house. Then I heard Salim call out, 'Oye, Sunil!'

I turned around. My joy knew no bounds. 'Oye, won't you come along?' Raju shouted.

I ran and joined them both. Aah! These were the people whom I knew well. My dear friends! The three of us sat by the fort. After a long time, and after talking about many things, I found out that Minakshi and Salim were no longer meeting each other. Neena, too, had drifted away from Raju because Minakshi had asked her to. Raju still kept talking about Neena very excitedly. He was happy with whatever he had experienced with her. Then, the three of us took an oath that we would never, ever let a girl interfere with our friendship. I was the loudest while taking this oath.

When I reached home, Father's English tuition was going on. Humming a song about true friendship, I went straight to the kitchen. I took some water out of the earthen pot, but before I could gulp it down, I realized there was a new face in the class. I kept the glass back near the pot and came out. In the corner, next to Father, sat Minakshi. I was astounded. She looked at me and smiled, and then started to look back into her notebook. Minakshi's smile conveyed that there was some secret conspiracy between the two of us. My heart began racing madly. Before I could go and take refuge in the kitchen, Father shot a question at me.

'Sunil, what's the Hindi word for "predictable"?' I kept staring at my father, and then I looked at my mother's black-and-white photograph. Several layers of dust had settled on the plastic garland around it. Minakshi's eyes were loaded with mischief, and I was quite predictable in this situation. I wanted to say there was no Hindi word for predictable.

'Come and sit here.' With a great degree of authority, Father commanded, so I went and sat next to Minakshi. My mind was occupied with predictable things. I knew what was to follow. Each time that Minakshi would come home for tuitions, I would keep going round and round in circles between the tuition room and the kitchen, like a hungry lion in a cage, but wouldn't say anything to her. The reason being not the oath that I had taken with my friends, but because I was a coward: fearful and predictable. I would never let Salim know that Minakshi now came to my house for tuitions. The simple reason for this was the deeply entrenched jealousy within me. I would find excuses to speak to my father during the tuitions, laced with heavy-duty English words. My father would assist me with this; after all, he was my father! I would not say the whole sentence, for I couldn't run the risk of faltering. Then one fine day, Minakshi could lose interest in English and this chapter, too, would end. And then, for years, I would keep thinking . . . what if! What if I had mustered enough courage to speak to Minakshi? Maybe the story would have been different.

Amidst the dilemma of these issues, I was pretending to be interested in learning from my father. Just then, Minakshi's hand touched mine. She wanted to give me a slip of paper, right there, in front of my father! I couldn't even imagine this. I quickly hid that slip under my feet and looked at Minakshi from the corner of my eye. There was that naughty smile on her lips. She was not looking at me, but she was aware that I was looking at her. Aah! My friendship! Salim, Raju . . . I was willing to put everything at stake for that one naughty smile. Love, indeed, turns a person into a cuckoo. My heart was racing. The slip of paper felt like a bomb under my feet. If Father found out about it, I would be in trouble. If I was predictable, then Minakshi was the extreme opposite of it. She was stretching the story and turning it towards a completely new direction. I wanted to read what was written in the slip immediately. But just like the mythological Angad, I refused to move my feet. In a while, the class was over, and Father went to the bathroom. Minakshi was slowly packing her bag. She was hanging around even after everyone else had left. When there was no one else in the room, I picked up that slip. It said, 'I know you are Pappu, but I am not Sonakshi; I am Minakshi. I will wait for your letter.' As the bathroom door clicked open, I put the slip in my mouth. After chewing on it a little, I swallowed it. By the time I stepped out of the house, Minakshi had already reached the end of the lane. Just before she turned, she looked back at me and then vanished. I began to coo, going round and round in circles, fixed to one spot.

Itti and Uday

She was sitting there yet again, on the same bench in the same park. Uday was holding her hand. Her lips were trembling, and her eyes were threatening to overflow. She wasn't blinking for the fear of her tears spilling out. But the tension was apparent on her face: right from her eyelids to the deep, dark circles under her eyes, and down to her lips. Despite the face being so tense, her ears were strangely normal. Perhaps they were used to listening to Uday's beating around the bush. The rest of her body wanted to break free and run away. It was experiencing a strange dullness.

Itti suddenly looked at Uday's hands. She had always liked his hands; the feeling still remained the same. His velvety palms and long, soft fingers: they had remained the same in this journey across the years. They were a constant during all the years in which she had attempted to come up with reasons to carry on with this relationship. The reasons were never enough. The relationship was unacceptable back then, and it still was. In fact, now, after all these years, there was nothing in it that even remotely resembled a relationship. Rather, it had turned into an ailment and Itti seemed to look for a cure for it each time she met with Uday.

She hadn't been intimate with Uday for more than a year now. She had said to him, right here in this park, on this bench, 'Uday, from now on, we shall only meet in this park.' It had been a momentary relief for her in this long-term disease.

Uday had always believed that he was a writer. He lived with the belief that he would, at some point, very soon, quit his construction business and finish his incomplete novel. Things had now reached a point where Itti had even stopped mentioning the novel. Earlier, she would call Uday a coward and a compromising person; but now, by the time she simply looked at Uday, he would already have changed the topic.

'Mili was asking about you. Do come home someday to meet her.'

In the middle of a random conversation, Uday suddenly mentioned his daughter.

'And what about Jiya?' Itti asked, looking straight into Uday's eyes.

'What about her? When does she have any time to spare from her TV serials?'

Uday said it so casually, as if he were talking about the weather. Itti had begun to find it quite funny. She wondered what kind of dialogues these were! There was no respite from them. Why do I have to face the same dialogues over and over again, she thought.

'How is Jiya?'

'Mili was insisting on meeting you.'

She thought to herself, 'Jiya is Uday's wife, and I am almost his keep. No, why am I embarrassed to admit it? I *am* his keep, his mistress!'

Itti looked at Uday's face. Her gaze paused at his lips, which were continuously moving. He was telling her some tale or the other. His other hand, the one that wasn't in Itti's, would make small actions at times. Words were pouring out from his mouth in a weird, whispered tone. If they were to remain seated here in this park for two days, Uday was quite capable of speaking non-stop the entire time. Earlier, she would lose herself in Uday's whispers and murmurs. His tales would create a strange whirlpool in which Itti would often get caught. Now, however, Uday kept talking while Itti remained hidden in her own self, searching for the original Itti who had probably tripped and lost herself long ago.

'We are done, Uday.'

She didn't realize when that sentence slipped out of her mouth.

'What?'

Uday was too deeply engrossed in his own tale to hear what she had said and asked, 'Did you say something?'

'No.'

Itti didn't even want to say 'no'. She simply wanted to shake her head, but this time, too, the word slipped out of her without seeking her permission.

'Itti, I was thinking of coming over to your place. It's been a long time since I met your mother. Let's go to your house and talk leisurely. Here, in the park, I get a strange and distant feeling, as if I don't know you.'

Itti was familiar with this play of words. When they met at home, it was for sex. When they met outdoors, it was to figure out a way to meet at home. But Itti had been particular about her decision not to meet at her home for the past one year. Every time Uday pleaded with her to invite him to her house, she said the same thing.

Just then a dried leaf came drifting down slowly from the tree. In this stillness, Itti was looking at the leaf's last flight. It fell into a pile of other dried leaves. Perhaps it was in a hurry to join the autumn, like all the other leaves. Yet, amongst all the other leaves, this leaf was different. Itti had spotted it. Her gaze was fixed on it. It kept flying here and there, yet Itti's gaze didn't stray even for a moment.

Suddenly, Itti began to feel that Uday was like that leaf, the one she felt was distinct from all the other leaves. These random meetings with Itti were what kept Uday distinct.

'Then what am I?' Itti began to think. 'Maybe my autumn lurks somewhere close by. And I am experiencing this restlessness for fear of getting lost in that autumn. This fear is what makes me seek Uday again and again. I am hoping that somehow, he will stop me from getting lost in the pile of autumn leaves.'

Itti gently removed her hand from Uday's. He was quiet. Maybe this was a silence after the end of a discussion; or the one just before he was about to begin a new one. Itti removed her hand when Uday was looking visibly tranquil. He looked at her questioningly, as if asking, 'Why did you remove your hand?' How could Itti answer that! She was already tired of all those questions to which no one had any answers. Instead, there were a lot of excuses. Initially, they both came up with excuses together. Eventually, they fashioned a game out of making paper planes from those excuses and then getting engrossed in playing with those planes.

'Uday, I am hungry. Can you get me something to eat?'

'Come, let's go somewhere and eat.'

Uday got up.

'A samosa, and, yes, some water, please.'

Itti's request sounded more like a stern command. So, when she did not get up from the bench to accompany Uday, he reluctantly said 'okay' and left to get what she had asked for.

Itti sighed deeply the moment he left. His presence was so heavy. The moment he left; she experienced the kind of relief a mountain climber feels when walking on ground level. She wanted to lie down on the bench for a while, yet she also wished to walk on this levelled ground for some time.

Itti walked away from the bench to the other side of the park. She had never come to this side of the park earlier. There were swings for children here which were not visible from the bench. There was a thick tree with dense foliage between the bench and these swings. However, the leaves were now falling. Itti could hear a little girl's laughter; she was on one of the swings. She saw a boy, perhaps her brother, who was pushing the swing for her. In the girl's laughter, Itti could sense a shivering that seemed to come from the fear of falling. The boy was using his entire body force to push the swing. Itti wanted to stop the boy. Just then, the shivers in the laughter ceased. Yet, at every ascent of the swing, the laughter became louder and louder. The boy had stopped pushing the swing. Its speed decreased gradually and, finally, it came to a halt. The boy ran and sat on another swing. The girl began to plead with him. She had started to enjoy the swinging and wanted to swing a little more. The boy had been interested in pushing her swing only while she had been scared. But the girl was still trying to please him. She was getting irritated, scolding him and crying at the same time, but he didn't budge. The girl slowly walked backed to the swing and sat on it. She remained seated there for a while quietly. Itti's lips felt parched, and her eyes began to burn. She decided she would push the swing, but her feet remained fixed, and she stood frozen. She felt as if this was a scene from some slow-moving play in which she was just a spectator. She could not get to the stage. Just then the little girl began to push with her feet, and gradually, the swing began to gather speed. The girl's laughter began to ring in Itti's ears. This time too there was fear in her laughter, but the fear was like a doorway into a house of joy that the girl had opened for herself. While swinging, laughter would enter that house like fresh air and the doorway of fear would shiver a little.

Hearing the girl's laughter, the boy left his swing and came to stand near her. But the girl was in a different world, oblivious to everyone around her. Each time she pushed with her feet, the swing went higher.

'Oh, you are here; I was looking for you all around in the park!'

Itti felt as if she had fallen off the swing.

'Did you bring water?'

Uday gave her the bottle and she nearly finished it in one go. They both started walking back towards the bench where they had been seated. Itti's was panting for breath, as if she had just come back running from somewhere.

'Uday, do you remember I used to like Raskolnikov?'

'Yes.'

Uday was carrying a packet of samosas in his hand. Itti threw away the empty bottle of water into a bin. In her thoughts, she was still sitting on the swing. She started to walk.

'Where are you going? Won't you sit?'

Itti had moved on. She didn't want to sit where they had been sitting previously.

'Let's sit on that bench further ahead,' she said. Itti wanted something else; something that she was experiencing within her.

'Why did you suddenly remember Dostoevsky?' Uday asked as he sat. He took out a samosa and offered it to Itti, but she shook her head.

'After committing a murder, we try to justify it with several reasons, and thereafter we commit many more murders, don't we?' This is what Itti wanted to say to Uday. Instead, she said, 'Just like that,' and ended the conversation. They both sat down on a bench from where Itti could see

---

* Protagonist from Fyodor Dostoevsky's novel *Crime and Punishment* (1866).

the swings clearly. The little girl was no longer there; only the empty swings were hanging by themselves.

Itti wanted to ask Uday about the girl. Where had she disappeared? Was she even actually there or had Itti imagined her? She looked at Uday. He was already engrossed in another tale of his. His lips were moving incessantly.

Having known a person over a period of time, we often do not feel the need for words for communication. Words become music; words lose their significance. Maybe it is this music that transported Itti to another world. Suddenly, she was reminded of that leaf which could not join the pile of autumn leaves. She couldn't see it anywhere; maybe it had finally merged into its autumn. Itti smiled a bit. She was still perched on that static swing. She began to notice things around the park. It was like an island of greenery in this concrete jungle. She couldn't recall the exact moment when she had first seen this park. Maybe it was on the first day of her job. She had stopped by to have a cup of tea that day just by the gate of this park; she had been with Uday. Until then, Itti and Uday had been good friends. The day Itti received her first salary was the day when they had first overstepped the boundaries of being just good friends. She had taken Uday out for dinner. In her salary cash, she had noticed a hundred-rupee note with the numbers 786 on it. Uday took that note from Itti and kissed it. He said, 'This is a sign of a new beginning; keep it safe.' She had; it was kept safely in the secret pocket of her purse.

Itti opened her purse and saw that note. It was there; constantly, as always!

'Uday, I want to take you out for dinner. Will you come with me?'

Uday was used to Itti getting excited on the spur of the moment. He never bothered to find out what kept her ticking. But he was happy at this proposal.

'Okay. But I will take you.'

'No, this one's on me. And we will go to the same hotel where we had our first dinner together. We will sit at the same place, the same table, and we will order the same dishes we had asked for that day. I want to give the waiter hundred rupees as a tip.'

'Hundred rupees as a tip to the waiter?'

'I should have given him a hundred rupees when we first dined there. Today, I will.'

Each time Itti remembered the hundred-rupee note with the lucky number 786 on it, she was reminded of 'we're done'. Uday, of course, had forgotten about that note long ago. He was talking about the highlights of that first dinner. Soon, he had reached the part about them getting physically intimate. For Itti, Uday's music had started, yet again! Suddenly, her foot pushed against the ground. With a squeaking sound, the swing had taken off. Listening to Uday's music, Itti felt a strong gust of wind blowing away all the dried autumn leaves. She was experiencing something like this for the first time. And then she saw herself come from somewhere and merge with the flying leaves. She saw herself dancing. The swing was going higher and higher and the sound of Itti's laughter reverberated with the wind.

The Copy Artist

My shins ache all the time: when I walk, when I am not walking, and even when I sleep. Today, when the pain didn't subside at all, I began to twist and turn my feet. After some oohs and aahs, the cramp-like feeling began to dissolve. That's when I called out to a passer-by and pleaded for help: 'Just press here so that this pain goes away.' He obliged me, and I cried out, 'Yes, this feels nice.' I kept pushing him; eventually, the man got tired and stopped pressing my feet. I felt drowsy, and he moved on. Experiencing some relief from the pain, a faint smile appeared on my face. I wanted to offer that passer-by a cup of tea, but he had already gone. I walked a few steps, and the pain returned with a vengeance. That's when I began to think that, perhaps, the pain was not in the body, but in the mind.

I am a victim of pain in the mind. I look for another passer-by, but I don't find anyone around me. Will I have to wait for the same passer-by who had pressed my feet a while ago and then moved on? Will he come back this way? Even if he does come back, will I tell him that my shins are aching? Perhaps I will tell him that the pain is, in fact, in my mind, so please press that. I wouldn't be surprised if he gets angry and begins to hit me.

It is so strange that the pain is in the mind and the discomfort is in the shins. So, when it is the shins that actually ache, will I feel the pain in the mind? The body is bigger than the soul. The physical body is everything that I am, at least, the way I think I am. In the journey of my life, whatever the cuts and curves, the ascents and descents . . . those are what my whole body is made up of. I have done nothing except walk along the path of life. In the process, I've left some scenes behind, hoping to see new ones. But the new scenes fill me with fatigue soon enough. In order to save myself from that fatigue, I begin to move forward. I never run. No, I won't ever run; I understood this long ago. My whole life finds purpose in looking for that one scene that will complete the picture. And the completion of it is my purpose in life. I knew this from the very beginning. Therefore, I stopped running long ago. As it is, I get very irritated with tourists. The kind of tourists who want to visit every place and see everything quickly, and then go and hide in their coops. I wonder, is this walking for many years the reason behind the ache in my shins? I haven't yet arrived at the scene that will complete my picture. So, what should I do? Should I halt? No, I shall wait. Either that same passer-by will come back, or the ache will cease to exist.

I have a friend named Suman. They have opened a women's bank in the neighbouring village and that is where she works. Due to the nature of her job at the bank, she has to always wear a saree: green, blue, brown . . . she looks very beautiful in a saree. On her days off from work, when I see her wearing a salwar-kameez, I feel as if her younger sister has come to meet me. And I am not just talking about her attire; her clothes affect her thought processes as well. For example, when wearing a saree, she always talks to me about lofty things: about the country, society, my tired life, revolution . . . But in a salwar-kameez, she immediately begins to talk about vegetables and groceries, or about watching a film.

She loves me. She thinks of love as a third person who lives with both of us. I always tell her that I won't be able to live with her alone, ever, because of this love. Earlier, she would laugh at such things; nowadays, she gets annoyed. One day she came to my room; she said it was oxygen-deprived and immediately opened all the doors and windows. And then suddenly, looking at my face, she said: 'Why is your face turning pale?' I said maybe it is because of the lack of oxygen. But she didn't agree. She insisted on taking me out. I refused, so she got annoyed and left. As soon as she left, I again shut all the doors and windows. I sat back on my bed and began to breathe heavily. The oxygen level in the room seemed fine to me. I could not understand the reason for my face losing its colour though.

There are three windows in my room. The first window has two panels; one opens into my mother's room and the other into my father's. The second window opens into my sister's room, and the third opens into the thick foliage of a tree. This window I never shut. I sometimes open the panel of the first window that opens into my mother's room. But the other panel, and the second window I mostly keep shut. That leaves just a door; I have no choice but to keep it shut. Because if I leave it open, I feel a nakedness that I cannot bear. I wake up early in the morning, exactly at the time when the sun is about to rise. That is the only time when I open the door to my house completely. After sunrise, I shut it. I have decided to open it only for social calls. Truth be told, I find sunrises very boring. But the time just before sunrise is surreal; it is different every day. It seems like the beginning of a play. What's more, a new technique is initiated each day. The sky, too, is a different colour every day—sometimes hazy, sometimes all clear. But as soon as the sun rises, it all becomes monotonous. It's the same predictable thing, day after day!

Social calls have nothing to do with the day's chitter-chatter. The noises that come from outside seem to be the ones from inside to me. Such as when my mother shouts, 'Food is ready,' she is actually my mother living inside the house with me who is gently saying, 'Food is ready, my child!' The banana-seller hawking outside is nothing but his coming indoors and resting with me for a brief while. Everything that is outside also exists in this room in the form of an echo. Whenever I step out of the house, I carry this room within me. The room lives within me with all its sounds, objects and corners. The moment I go out, the room turns into a bag that keeps in itself whatever it sees, as if *it* is out shopping.

Nowadays, whenever I am outdoors, I keep looking for mirrors. Ever since Suman pointed out that my face was losing its colour, I have developed this habit of looking into every mirror. While some mirrors reflect back a clear face, in some I can see my paleness. It is prominent on the forehead and not so visible in the rest of my face. Is it related to the pain in my mind? Or is it related to the ache in my shins?

In the evening, I stepped out of the house to take a stroll and to eat golgappas. As a ritual, I definitely eat golgappas at Saroj's cart in the evening, twice a week. Saroj and I chat for hours. He sets up shop at 5 p.m. After arranging his cart, he removes his shirt, hangs it in a corner of the cart, and begins work in his vest which is torn in many places.

'I am seeing you after so long!' He said this out of a habit; many days could mean a single day, or actually more days.

'There is a pain in my mind, but I feel the discomfort in my shins,' I said to Saroj.

'Eat golgappas,' he replied.

'Do you find my face pale?'

'There are no potatoes today. Will gram do?'

'When you say, "I am seeing you after so long!", does that mean you have been waiting to see me?'

'I accidentally added extra tamarind to the water today,' he said, and handed me a small plate.

I returned home after eating the golgappas. Does Saroj actually wait for me? If I don't go to his cart for many days, many months, many years, will he come home to ask me why I haven't visited his shop? Perhaps he will glance once or twice at the road that I take to come to his cart. Maybe.

I haven't gone to work for the last ten days. Just as I hear a knock on the door and I walk towards it, I sense this feeling of waiting. Though I do not know for whom, but I am certainly waiting for someone. This is either someone I don't know or someone I want to know.

Leaving aside the social calls, do I sit at home and wait anyway? I am happy to see Suman when she comes by, but I don't wait for her. I have never said to her, 'I am seeing you after so long!' even when she actually visits after many days. To whom do I want to say this sentence? Whenever I walk around the house, with all the doors and windows closed, there is always someone for whom I wait. But for whom? I wait for someone about whom I don't know myself. This thought is stuck obstinately in my mind. I thought I would ask Suman, but will she be able to answer my question? When I myself don't know, how will she?

The pain in the shins has suddenly worsened. I shouldn't have gone today to have the golgappas. I lie down in my bed. I have to go to work tomorrow.

I work at a shop where they make copies of everything. I make good copies: of books, photos, paintings and people. I am mostly assigned to copy portraits of faces, which I am good at. People often come to me with black-and-white photos of their parents and ask for them to be turned into coloured images. So, apart from copying images, I also make coloured portraits out of black-and-white photos. But when someone demands that their mother should have a smiling face in the portrait I make, even though she looks angry in the original photo, I get annoyed. Why should I forcibly paste a smile on somebody's face? No, that I don't do.

A strange incident took place a few days ago, due to which I had to take ten days' leave from work. This was around the same time that my shins had begun to hurt badly. A woman approached me. She wanted to get her husband's portrait made. I asked if the husband was no more. She lost her temper when I asked her that. I tried to calm her down by explaining that people often asked for portraits of those who had passed away. Finally, she took out a picture of her husband and showed it to me. He looked like a smiling, happy-go-lucky fellow. I told her to collect the portrait the following week; the price was settled at Rs 2500.

When she came to collect the portrait, she got annoyed again. She saw it and started to argue with me. The dispute reached the owner. He, however, liked the portrait. But the woman said, 'Look at his face carefully. Doesn't it seem that behind his smile lies some hidden pain, some sadness. Look at his forehead . . .' Hearing this, the owner asked me to identify where the person in the portrait seemed to have pain. I immediately blurted out that his shins were hurting. The woman got so angry that she left without taking the portrait. And I was told to go on leave till the pain in my shins got cured. What's more, I was informed that I owed the owner Rs 1700 now. I took leave of absence for ten days and went home after paying Rs 900 to the owner. The pain in the shins continued. I know that the pain isn't in the shins but in the mind.

As an artist, I had some questions about the portrait incident. So, when I went to return the money to the owner,

I asked, 'Sir, the pain was in my shins, the man's face had a smile, alright; yet, there was some pain somewhere, and that was evident. So, wasn't the portrait more alive than the photograph?'

'No,' he replied.

'How is that possible? There must be some difference between clicking a picture and making a portrait!'

'No. Only if you bring your personal tensions to your work will there be a difference. If you leave them behind at home, there won't be any difference.'

'But . . . I . . .'

'Don't talk about art and the artist. You owe me Rs 1700; first pay that.'

The conversation ended at the mention of money. When I told Suman about the whole affair, she was quite angry.

'That owner is stupid; he doesn't value your talent. Leave the job . . . you are an artist . . .'

I remained quiet for some time, and then said softly, 'No, I can't do that.'

Suman became quiet, and I began to pace up and down the room.

'I am good at my work. The owner knows that, and that's why he has not dismissed me from the job. Moreover, what else can I do? I only know how to imitate. Copy this, copy that! Show me Amitabh Bachchan's expression when he gets angry . . . show me an elephant or a lion . . . I can copy all of that. That's all I know.'

Suman disagreed. She always believes me to be someone else; something other than what I am. I keep telling her I

am not that someone else, but she doesn't listen. Well . . .
she has a reason. Once, when I was home for a few days,
I had randomly made some paintings of Suman. From my
window, I have always seen her walk back and forth by
the tree on the road. So, in my paintings, I painted her
many sarees in between the leaves of the tree. Suman was
delighted to see them. I tried to tell her that even these
paintings were an imitation of the real—an imitation of
the moments I had experienced standing by the window,
watching her. But she again disagreed. I gave all those
paintings to Suman. Since then she feels I am, in reality,
someone else, and not who I really am—the copy artist.

One day I had asked the golgappa-seller, 'Listen, Saroj,
am I exactly the same person that I look like?' After a long
silence, Saroj said, 'I will have to buy a new pitcher; the
water doesn't stay cool in this one for long.'

Concealing the pain in my shins, I reached my place of
work. There was a lot of pending work due to my ten days'
leave. Avoiding the owner's gaze, I slipped into the storage
room. Even though there were a lot of people like me who
worked for him, yet there were some tasks that only I could
perform. So, I got engrossed in my work. The pain in the
shins—which I had clearly established as the pain in my
mind—was increasingly constantly. In about a week, I
completed all the pending work. It was Sunday, and I spent
Sundays with Suman. We would usually sit around in some
temple on Sundays. Though I did not believe in any God,
yet I appreciated the serenity inside temples, especially the
Kale Mahadev temple by the riverside. Its floor was cool
even at noon. Suman and I would sit there for hours.

Suman usually wore a salwar-kameez on Sundays, but today she was wearing a saree. Therefore, her conversations were heavy-duty and mature. After being silent for some time, I ended up talking about the constant pain in my shins. This was completely unintentional. Suman was quiet for a while, and then said something about pressing my legs. To which I said, 'Not legs. The pain is in the mind, and the discomfort extends to the shins.'

'I hope you don't have jaundice?' she said, brushing aside the hair from my forehead. I showed her my nails. It wasn't jaundice.

'Your face is growing paler by the day.' Her sentence was full of concern and worry.

The cause for this, too, was the pain in my mind, but I was unable to explain this to Suman. After a while, she pulled out a coconut from the folds of her saree. I was to go and make the offering because women were not allowed to go inside the Kale Mahadev temple. After doing so, we set out to circumambulate the temple seven times. Suman had covered her head and was mumbling something while walking. What was she saying to Kale Mahadev in whose temple she wasn't even permitted to enter? After finishing the circumambulations, we took a stroll across the ghat and then returned home.

Before I went to sleep, on Sunday night, I kept thinking about Suman. We had spent several Sundays at the Kale Mahadev temples. At times, she would wear a saree, and at other times a salwar-kameez. The priest at the temple had begun to recognize us. He presumed that we were married. Sometimes, he would even offer us some tea. One day he walked up to Suman, put his hand on her head in a gesture of blessing, and said, 'Child, don't worry, you will have a child, soon. Kale Baba answers everyone's prayers.' I remained quiet but Suman held his hand and started to cry, as if that is what she had always prayed for at the temple.

I tried to ask her many times the reason for her crying, but never had the courage to actually do so. Suman loved to talk about the future a lot. Whenever she wore a salwar-kameez, the future seemed prosperous and full of possibilities. It was the salwar-kameez that made her talk about the future as if she were in some gaming zone and had just one minute to gather as many points as she could. But when she wore a saree, the future seemed like a mountain; a thorny mountain on which each step had to be placed carefully. Even the slightest carelessness could lead to certain death. Though I never understood whose death: of our dream of a future, of our relationship, her death or perhaps mine? Irrespective, I loved to hear about the future.

When I reached work the following day, the owner called for me. I came to understand that my week-long hard work had all been a waste. All my paintings showed pain. I was shown all the portraits that I had painted in the past week. Almost all of them displayed pain on their faces, somewhere close to the forehead. There was another strange thing: most of the portraits from the last week had yellow as the dominant colour. In some, I had only used yellow. The owner didn't ask any questions this time. He simply called me a 'notorious artist' and dismissed me from service. As I was leaving, he handed over a slip of paper on which was written the amount that I owed him now: Rs 17,000. Looking at the slip, the pain in my shins suddenly increased. I almost crawled back home.

I don't know anything except how to copy. At home, I kept wondering about what other things I could copy. What else could I do? I could not come up with anything. I had to return Rs 17,000; this thought was tiring me out. The whole thing had begun with pain in the shins and had now reached the pain in the mind; to top it all, there was now the paleness of my face. One fine day, I went and sat at the Kale Mahadev temple all by myself. The river was flowing at its usual pace. Kale Mahadev remained at the same place, with lots of coconuts around. The priest passed me by twice or thrice but refused to recognize me since I was alone. It made me feel as if I had no identity without Suman.

Sitting in the temple, I had a strong urge to imitate something; to imitate everyone—Kale Mahadev, the lonely moments I had spent by my window, the closed windows, Suman, the shop owner, the golgappa-seller . . . everyone—imitate everything. I bought a whole lot of colours and canvasses, and on reaching my room, bolted it from the inside.

My life is not dependent in the search of the scene that would complete the painting. Rather, my whole being exists to create that very painting. It has no end, just like it had no beginning. So, the day I finish my painting, I won't be around to see it. I came to this realization much later.

The Swallow

If you say so . . . I'll try once again to love you
from the beginning.
I'll again give you every ache of our gazes meeting now and
then. As I follow you, I will stop you
in some corner of your lane.
But I won't be able to say anything.
Each day I will tell you of a dream that I never dreamt.
But if you give me one more chance,
this time I won't take a false oath
that the dream was true.
However, I will also not give you the entire picture at once.
Instead, I will give you just a taste
of the syrup of lies . . .

'Stop it. I don't want to listen to this,' she said, getting up from the chair. Just a while ago, she had insisted on listening to something. I fell silent, and she started to pace up and down the room. She was overwhelmed by her own being; she was seeking a corner where she could disappear. She wanted to be lost in a way that she became a part of this house. Just like the chair from which she had just risen.

'What happened?' I asked, changing my voice. It wasn't the voice in which I was reciting my poem.

'There is a strange stink in your poems nowadays; I don't know what or whose . . .'

Maybe she had found a corner, and she had held on to that, regained her composure, and then said this. To me, she had not become an object; she seemed like a brand-new thing brought into the house. While all the things in my house can be described as 'old' and 'messed up', she seems new . . . clean . . . washed. It is not as if there is nothing new in my house; they simply become a part of the house over time. So much so that even a new book joined the older ones. But she—despite visiting me for the last one year, in spite of being read—has not grown old. Even though I have been attempting to merge her with the whole house.

'I can't do much about trying to find your being . . . in my writing.' I had been murmuring this to myself for a long time, and then I said it aloud with the seriousness befitting a writer.

It was late at night; the thought of dropping her back to her house and the laziness associated with it almost killed the joy of her being there. She never stayed the night at my house. After I repeatedly asked her the reason for it, she said that she could only sleep in her own bed.

She was silent about what I had just said. Despite the dim light from the only lamp in the corner, her presence was clearly visible—not fully, but at least her bright face and long, white hands. I suddenly thought of a peculiar little bird I had seen in the Chaukodi village in Uttarakhand. Swallows—very small and beautiful—had made their nests in small little shops in the village. Initially, I found the bird to be strange, nesting inside those dark and cold shops, almost like a colourful, decorative bindi on an old, wearied and wrinkled face. However, later, I would go into those shops only to see the bird which had become the most interesting and worthwhile aspect of the shops.

'I know this is my imagination and nothing more, but I feel you are cheating on me. No, not cheating, but something else. Last night, when we were intimate, it felt like you were thinking of someone else. You were touching me but imagining someone else instead. But then I also realized that these are probably all my insecurities and nothing else. But right now, listening to the poem, I was again reminded of it. I do not want an answer for this; I just wanted to let you know.'

At this hour of the night, her words seemed to be coming out slower than their actual pace, and also seemed heavier. I felt as if I was reading them, not listening to them.

'No, these are not insecurities; if you actually consider this to be cheating, then, yes, I'm actually cheating you. Even right now, as you stand in that corner, I am thinking about someone else.'

I couldn't tell her that at that time I was actually thinking about the swallow. I don't know why, but I should have said it.

'I want to ask you one more thing . . . when you are with me, how long do you stay with me?'

'All the time.'

'That's a lie.'

'Honestly.'

'You are lying.'

'See, the thing is . . .'

'I don't want to listen to anything. I am leaving.'

'I will drop you off. Wait.'

'No need.'

She left, and I continued sitting in the empty room with the half-recited poem and the frustration of having put forward only half my point. I thought of reciting the rest of the poem to the old, scattered things of my house but I couldn't gather the courage. Since I hadn't gone along to drop her home this evening, the comfort of her having been here was still with me. Was I really thinking about someone else while I was intimate with her last night? Whom was I thinking about?

Yes, I remember now. When I was running my fingers over her face, I was reminded of the morning when, after cremating my mother, I was collecting her bones from the ashes, as required by ritual. When I had touched her nose, it seemed like the only bone I could find in the ashes of my mother. I had kept moving my hand in one part of the ash, pretending to find more bones, because honestly, I didn't want to touch any more of my mother's bones. The instant I found one, I would start wondering which part of her body that bone belonged to. This was even more traumatic than her death. Then I began to think about how I would feel if

I had to look for her bones after cremating her . . . and with this thought I moved my hand towards her back. It seemed as if she had been cremated, that her body was ash, and I was searching for her bones. She started laughing but I was serious; because I was actually searching for her bones.

She is right; when I am looking at her, I am actually thinking about other things.

I switched off the table lamp, but the darkness in the room became unbearable. So, I switched it on again. Sleep had become such a strange habit. Because of her presence, my nights had their own small rituals, and without completing those, I couldn't sleep. Like dropping her home and coming back to an empty house, and then trying to find the sorrow of the joy of togetherness. I would immediately put it all down on paper after returning home.

It is rather strange that when I was going through my toughest phase, I was writing about the beauty of life; and when I was finally beginning to experience happiness and peace at home, I was gathering the sorrow of writing about pain. Perhaps this is the reason that I think or write about someone else who could have been here instead of her, whenever she visits me. Yesterday, after dropping her, I came back and wrote the poem that she did not want to listen to. Other rituals included playing the music that I wanted to hear while she was here, immediately after I entered the house, took off my clothes and threw away all the adornments of being a man, playing with sleep till it didn't checkmate me, then drinking tea, brushing my teeth and at times, taking a bath, too.

Neither did I go to drop her home, nor did I begin with the rituals for the night. Instead, I began to think again about the swallow. A man from the same village—Chaukodi—had told me that the bird found mention in the Quran; that it collects specks of dust while flying and then makes its nest by spitting those out. I contemplated listening to music; then considering that the whole night was ahead of me, I decided to make some tea first. I had just entered my kitchen to make tea when I heard the doorbell. I opened the door to see her standing outside. Before I could say anything, she swiftly walked in.

'Couldn't you come to placate me? You know I can't go home alone; I feel scared.'

I was not aware of this. I didn't even know that she could walk away, so her coming back was also as new for me as her going off suddenly. In both the situations, what was the right way to behave, I didn't know. I kept sitting quietly for some time. Then, quite contrary to my normal behaviour, I went and sat by her side.

'I am sorry. Forgive me.'

This admission was as true as it was clever. Even though it was not directed towards appeasement, yet she imagined it to be so and was placated. She turned towards me and smiled and started playing with my hair.

'Do you remember when we first met? I thought you were a loser who was annoyed with everyone. What did you say your age was at that time, thirty-five? Right?'

'We met only a year ago. I was forty-three last year.'

'All right, forty-four! How does a year or two make a difference?' She was laughing. But I knew she was provoking me. Had the circumstances been different, I would not have replied. I wanted to reply now because I wanted to divert her from the topic of me being a loser. Her fingers left my hair.

'After forty, every single year makes a difference,' I said, subduing a smile.

'Yes, you are right.'

Saying this, she burst into laughter and the whole room echoed with its sound. Unable to understand what the joke was, I chose to stay quiet. Once she had calmed down, her hands moved towards my hair again. Her caressing felt as if she was searching for something.

'When I was younger, we used to have a lot of gatherings at our home.'

Now she struck a new note. She started caressing my hands as if whatever she was saying was written on them.

'My father was very fond of conversations and debates. I was always the apple of everyone's eye at those gatherings. Whenever I was ignored, I would start throwing temper tantrums and behave strangely. I would break crockery, cry, and once I even slashed my wrist. I said it was an accident, but till date no one knows that I did it deliberately. Even now, it is my favourite pastime to hallucinate about having met with an accident or falling very sick, and people coming to enquire about my health. When I broke up with Ashish, I used to think about my death, and derived great pleasure imagining how remorseful he would feel; that he would cry and bang his head in grief, but I would be dead. Do you understand what I am saying?'

'Yes.'

I had simply wanted to say 'hmmm' but I blurted out a 'yes'. I liked it when she talked like this. These stories of hers, in which there was only the female protagonist and no one else. As soon as her role got over, it was the end of the story.

'You will find it strange that now I get irritated by children who try to seek attention. I often get angry at work too. I hate people who indulge in self-pity. Maybe I am trying to make amends for my past behaviour . . .'

'Hmmm . . .'

'What does your "hmmm" mean? I actually feel so!'

I didn't want to get trapped in a conversation. So, I was simply responding with a 'hmmm' or a 'yes'. After a while, though, I said, 'I am amazed at how you can speak the truth so simply and candidly while I fill pages and pages with my stories in an attempt to speak the truth. Aren't you getting late?'

'Do you want to go to sleep?' she retorted immediately. Perhaps she wanted to ask if I was getting bored. No, I wasn't getting bored, but I was scared about any further mention of that loser that she said I was.

'No, in fact, I was going ask if you would like to have a drink.'

'I would love a glass of wine.'

'I don't have wine right now.'

'Then why did you ask!'

'Well . . . there is rum, whisky, even tea.'

'Some tea would be nice.'

'Sure?'

I had first met her about a year ago. She had not read any of my writing, and yet had asked me some questions about it. I was irritated with her at our very first meeting itself. Thereafter, she called and said, 'This is Aarti speaking.' Since this was the first time she was telling me her name, on the phone, I failed to recognize her. She continued, 'I have written a story. I want to read it out to you.'

I recognized her only when she came home, and I instantly regretted calling her over. Anyway, now I was stuck! I was simply going to listen to the story and let her go; at least that was the plan. As soon as she started reading out her story, I wanted to laugh. The title of the story was 'I am a mere thought'. The story was full of phrases like 'the world could not understand me'. She could not speak Hindi fluently, yet the whole story was full of words that made me feel embarrassed about my Hindi. Somehow the story-reading session got over, and soon after, she began to cry. I could not understand what was happening. I tried to console her while staying within my limits, that is, without touching her, but she continued to sob. Unwittingly, and unwillingly, I was a witness to childish behaviour. I was apprehensive of a dialogue in which she would divulge the reason for her crying. Yet, I knew she wanted to tell me.

'Actually, I wrote this story because . . .' she started. I intuitively knew that she was going to begin right from her birth. Since this would have consumed a large chunk of my time, I interrupted her.

'Listen, I don't want to hear why you have written this story. I give more importance to the story itself—the written part—rather than the reason why it was written.'

'No, but this is my story, and I want to tell you why it is written the way it is.'

As if wanting to narrate her pain quickly, she began to speak fast but I stopped her.

'See, what a writer does, or how an artist lives, and what he thinks—their personal life—isn't important at all. What is significant is what he is capable of expressing through his art. I had a friend who used to admire a certain poet's poems which were quite intense. But when she met the poet in person, she was so disappointed that she stopped reading his writings altogether. This is wrong. These are always two different people: the one who writes, and the other who lives just like everyone else.'

I felt that, by diverting the topic of conversation so skilfully, I had also dealt with the issue of our first meeting in which she had called me pessimistic, and I had been shying away from listening to her talk about it.

As a consequence of my not listening to her reasons behind writing her story, she started to frequent my place. I realized that much more than her needing me, it was I who had gotten used to her coming over. I still haven't heard her out; she still tries to bring it up in casual conversations, but I always snub her. As a result, I have begun to fear that the day she tells me her reasons for writing her story, she will stop coming over. She has never written a story after the first one, but she has composed some brief poems which have never been recited to me. I have simply been informed that a poem has been composed the previous day. On my part, I have never encouraged her to recite them to me.

The tea was ready. I brought it out of the kitchen and saw that she had dozed off while sitting in the chair. I gently placed the teacup by her side and extended my hands towards her shoulders to wake her up but stopped. Her eyes were shut, and there was a faint smile on her lips, as if she was narrating a very interesting incident. I sat beside her, and for no reason at all I began to think about her story. Why must she have written that story? I began feeling guilty for not wanting to listen to her reasons for writing her story. How frightened I was of any kind of responsibility! Yes, this would have been a kind of responsibility . . . to know about someone's reasons for doing something. The same way that no matter how involved you are in any kind of a relationship with a girl, the moment you meet her parents, you begin to feel a sense of responsibility; not towards her, but towards her parents.

I took my cup of tea and stood beside the window. It was quiet outside. Every once in a while, a vehicle could be seen on the road. The sky was studded with stars and a calm breeze was blowing. I turned around to look at her; she was still asleep. Looking at her, my thoughts went back to the swallow. I began to imagine that my house was a shop in that hilly village and that it was filled with darkness. And in this shop-like house, she was a swallow. She could never be a part of this house; she could never be the wrinkles on the worn-out face of this old house. But she could always be like a bindi on that face. In fact, she *was* the bindi of my house, and this thought brought forth such immense love in my heart for her that I wanted to wake her up, calling her my swallow; I even wanted to ask her the reasons for writing her story. I wanted to embrace her and tell her that she was my bindi, the bindi of my house.

'What are you looking at?' she asked suddenly.

I was startled.

'Oh! I thought you were asleep.'

'That isn't the answer to my question.'

I could not see her eyes in the faint light of the table lamp; it seemed like she was still asleep, and this was someone else speaking, not her.

'I was looking at you. You were looking so beautiful.'

This sentence was full of suspicion, fear. Maybe she was still asleep. Because it is unlikely that I would have said this to her while she was awake. I felt I had been caught red-handed while stealing, and I couldn't bear to stand there anymore. I went close to her. Sitting on the edge of the chair, I hastily entangled my fingers in her hair and began to caress it. She smiled. The moment she smiled, it felt like someone else was the thief and had been caught near the window. I was not the thief; I was simply the one who was caressing her hair. Thinking on these lines, I began to smile too.

After a while, I dropped her home, just like I always did. She had forgotten to have the tea I had made; I noticed it when I returned home. While returning, I couldn't think about anything else but her. Yes, in between I thought about the swallow, too. This took me to the hills, but I didn't want to go to the hills as of now. So, I didn't keep that thought for long. I didn't have to struggle with sleep after returning, and the moment I got into bed it engulfed me.

In a few days, I had to travel. When I returned after almost two weeks, she was gone. I did not enquire much about her; it was not that I didn't want to meet her. Call it my laziness or the realization that this relationship could last only this long. I let go. I didn't have anything more to give to her and she didn't have anything left other than her reasons for writing her story. Had she stayed in the same city, we would have erased the boredom of our meetings with a phase of not meeting. And then once again, the same sequence of events would have begun. Of course, this, too, was my imagination.

After many months of this episode, I wrote a poem titled 'The Swallow'. It was published in a Hindi magazine along with the half-poem that I had recited to her. I did this on purpose . . . publishing both the poems together. In the hope that she would read them someday and maybe she would know whom I was thinking about that night when we were together.

Night in the Hills

Sipping my tea, for a while now, I was watching the surprising incidents taking place in front of me. In this small village in the mountains, where the tea shop was located, some clouds had drifted by rather suddenly. A light drizzle had followed even as the two mountains in the background were still sunny. Now, a bright golden daze had encased everything.

The shop where I am having tea belongs to an elderly couple. This is probably the only shop in a radius of about three kilometres. The couple, it appears, live by themselves. They say they have a farm in the village in the valley below which is managed by two of their children. Two of their daughters are married and a son studies somewhere in Delhi, they proudly tell me. Since there is no other shop nearby, this tea shop also serves as a basic groceries store. After having almost three full cups of tea, I notice the intense fog making its way towards us from behind the smaller mountains. The couple are busy with their work. I shout, 'Look! The fog looks so endearing!'

They give a cursory glance at the fog and go back to work. I begin clicking pictures. Through the lens of the camera, I see a small white dot. I move my eye away from the lens and see an old man walking towards us from some village down below. He is quick for his age and reaches the shop quick quickly. Soon he is engaged in a conversation with the couple in their native language. So, I start looking at the mountains again. It seems like someone has lit a huge bonfire right behind that small mountain, and the smoke is making its towards us. In a short while, the tea shop and the entire village is enveloped in that cloud of fog. The shopkeeper says, 'The fog has a fragrance of its own.' When I ask what kind of fragrance, he says if I lived there longer, I would know.

I realize it is five in the evening already, and I have to travel about eight to nine kilometres to reach my guest house. The thought of walking alone in the night in this forest sends a shiver down my spine. The shopkeeper almost smells my fear and says that I could walk back with the old man. He says he lives in the same village where my guest house is located. I readily agree. I pick up my bag and wait for the old man to get up. He remains seated and asks for a cup of tea. I look at my watch. I know that the old man had casually glanced at me when he had entered the shop, after which he was either chit-chatting with the shopkeeper or staring blankly at nothing. As a tourist, you expect to be looked at; people look for reasons to talk to you and soon you get used to the attention. But this old man has simply overlooked my presence in the shop. I am beginning to feel angry now; the kind of anger I had felt when I first saw a lion in a cage. It was caged and I was standing right in front of it, yet the lion behaved as if I didn't exist or was completely transparent. I started shouting at that lion, did some antics, but it paid no heed at all. My friends said I looked like a monkey in front of the lion.

When the old man slowly begins sipping his tea, I put my bag down loudly enough to express my anger about the long wait he is putting me through. I do not show much anger because I do not want to behave like a monkey again. I too order for more tea. The lady of the shop gives me a long lecture about having too much tea. I step out of the shop, finish my tea, pay for the old man's cup as well as mine. He looks at me once and doesn't even smile; a 'thank you' is probably too much to expect.

Anyway, after about half an hour, we start our journey, the old man and me. It is half past five, and the sun has disappeared. The old man is leading the way. I ask him his name. Thrice. He says nothing and we keep walking. In a while it begins getting darker. I take out a torch from my bag and hold it in my hand for a while. Then I slowly switch it on to ensure it is working properly. As soon as I switch it on, he says, 'Keep it inside.' I say, 'It's too dark. We won't be able to see the path.' He does not reply. I switch off the torch, but because he didn't reply, I don't put it back in my bag; I keep holding on to it. Then he says slowly, 'A torch is not required here. Keep it inside. If you keep holding it in your hands, you will be tempted to switch it on.' His voice feels heavier as the night progresses.

I am surprised that his Hindi has no accent. He is speaking proper Hindi. I put the torch into my bag. Had I been alone, even with a torch, I wouldn't have been able to stand this darkness, I think to myself. At least in his company I was less fearful.

During the day, the same forest had appeared so beautiful to me that I could have wandered in it for hours. Now at nightfall it has transformed into something ghoulish and scary. Oh! Why I am thinking so, I curse myself. Suddenly, there is a slight sound from the top of the mountain. I cannot gather enough courage to even look that way. I take a couple of long strides and begin walking right next to the old gentleman, almost clinging to him. I don't want to say anything, but the words slip out of my mouth, and that, too, in a weird tone, 'How long will it take us to reach the village?'

The night falls suddenly, as if someone had switched off a light bulb. To be honest, at this moment I am not scared of either the darkness or the forest. I am not even scared of the strange noises around us. I am only scared of the old man who is unresponsive to my queries. He should have told me right when we started from the tea shop that he did not like talking on the way. This eerie silence is intimidating me. I start walking slightly away from him. I am glancing intermittently at him and the intense darkness. His silence is creating such a scary ambience in this dark quiet night that it is almost unbearable. I am so fearful that I begin to imagine strange things—like the old man might turn around and tell me that he lives on this tree, that I must now go ahead alone . . . and then he would climb the tree and begin to laugh eerily. I would die that very second. I immediately look at his feet and realize with relief that they are straight. Yes, I know, this is all so childish. But had it been anyone else in my situation, especially someone as cowardly as I, they, too, would have thought the same weird thoughts.

At a distance is the flickering light of a bulb that will be invisible as soon as we take a turn. But somehow, we are not getting any closer to that bulb. Suddenly, I feel that this man is taking me around in circles. The end of the road seems nowhere. I wonder if it took me so long during the day. Gathering some courage, I ask again, 'How far now?' In this pin-drop silence, my own voice seems so loud that I swallow back the latter half of my sentence. You won't believe it, but he still remained quiet. An inner voice suggests that I start running for my life, but I continue following him. Not bothered about the darkness surrounding us, I am only focusing on him.

This time I clear my throat and collecting all my fearful confidence together, I ask, 'Mister, how much more time will it take us?' This time he looks at me. I avoid his gaze out of fear. When I look at him again, he is back to walking at his regular pace, gazing blankly into the darkness ahead. I am almost dead now. Either he ought to say something, or I will die of intimidation. Even though he has a stick in his hand, he is not using it as a walking stick. His steps are soundless. I think of snatching the stick, hitting him with it on his head and running away.

Suddenly, there is a voice, his voice, indeed. 'Are you listening?' I didn't understand. 'Yes?' That is all I can utter.

'These little noises, this rhythm. Can't you hear them? This is the existence of the night.' I am quiet. His speech has a strange music to it. 'The village is close by now,' he says softly and then goes back to being quiet. It is as if someone behind me is tugging at my fear. The village is close by—this sentence works like a consolation prize for me. I am now less scared and not thinking too badly about him. Suddenly, he stops. Without saying a word, he climbs downhill next to the path.

The feeling that he is about to climb a tree returns. I am standing absolutely alone on the dark path. I say softly, 'Mister, where have you gone?' I then use some more forms of address, say a few broken sentences, and then quieten down. Half the fear that I had left behind comes back and clings to me again. I start looking all around me. I slide my hand slowly into my bag and take out my torch. I am about to switch it on when I hear him urinate. I don't switch it on. Instead, I stand closer to the path from where he had descended downhill. The sound of him urinating stops but he doesn't come up. I try peering towards where he had disappeared but can't see anything. I switch on my torch and look around. Nothing. The beam of light from the torch is making the darkness seem even scarier. I shout, 'Dada! Daddu! Bhai Saheb! Are you all right?'

Suddenly, a voice emerges from a few steps ahead. 'Let's go. Why are you standing there?' When did he walk past me? I shine my torch on him and a strange feeling overcomes me. He is looking very scary standing at a distance; I don't have the courage to walk up to him. I switch off the torch and begin taking fast strides towards him. He is looking at me. As I approach him, I feel he is about to do something. I can sense the preparedness of a hunting lion in his eyes; the way it looks at its prey one last time before pouncing on it. I am shaking and so I start running towards him. He doesn't move and so I push him aside. He falls down. I don't stop running till I reach my guest house. It all happens so quickly. When I am about to fall asleep in my room, that's when I think of the old man. I stay awake for a long time that night but don't have the courage to leave my room. I decide to enquire about him in the morning.

I reach the spot in the morning. I wonder how I could have been scared of this serenity the previous night. I try to look for the old man, but he is nowhere to be seen. I return to the village. I don't feel like going inside the guest house and so I go to a tea shop and ask for a cup of tea.

I start reading the papers. Suddenly, I see a man passing by with a small child. To my amazement, I realize that it is the man from last night. He looks at me for a second, averts his gaze and resumes walking. I want to apologize to him. I call out to him once, twice, but he doesn't look back. The child walking with him does look back at me once. The tea seller interjects, 'That is Dyunda.' I start to call him by his name; the tea seller interrupts me again and tells me that he is deaf.

I tell the tea seller that he was with me last night, and I didn't realize that he couldn't hear. I do not waste any more time in that discussion. My guilt is weighing me down. I leave my tea and run up to him. When I stand in front of him, he stops. I gesture an apology, but he keeps looking at me in amazement as if he doesn't remember anything. I fall at his feet. I then buy a handful of toffees from the nearby shop for the child accompanying him. I come back and stand in front of him and don't move. I want my apology to be accepted. Slowly, a faint smile touches his eyes and then his lips, as if he had read all about last night in my eyes. I heave a sigh of relief at his smile and step aside. He resumes walking with the child.

Five Grains of Sugar

Now I smile in a particular way
And I laugh in a certain way too.
Yes, I have learnt how to survive.
Now I see everything as it appears. Whatever isn't visible
doesn't exist for me and I am least bothered.
I walk the middle path.
I leave home every day, and I return. Nothing affects me.
Suffice it to say that
my tongue has lost its sense of taste.
Now everything appears white to me. I don't know
anything,
but I carry a know-it-all expression on my face. I know
how to laugh and sigh at every story told. Now I am happy;
no, not happy; now I am tranquil . . . peaceful . . .
Because now I only want to remain alive. Neither do I fly,
nor do I flow now;
Have I stagnated?

Whatever you think of it, I have become indifferent.
Now I am real, almost real.
Let me place my head in my imagination and sleep.
I want to see that world whose reflection this world is.
All this seems meaningless now. My reality laughs at my
own old fantasies now.
Oh, yes! Nowadays I, too, laugh a lot.
At times I feel this laughter is an ailment
and I laugh at this thought.
Now everything is where it is supposed to be. All this feels
extremely good.
Not good, okay . . . yes, it seems okay.
But . . . there is a problem; a strange, incomplete one . . .
what do I say?
I don't cry these days; sounds strange, doesn't it? Neither
happiness nor sadness affects me. Because whenever they
arrive,
they are satisfied by a mere sigh or a laugh.
It is strange!
No, no . . . this isn't strange.
It is a strange feeling,
as if you are dead and no one believes it. People talk to you
as a routine,
offer you tea, wander around with you
and only you know that you aren't alive now
I know, this is a depressing thought
and that you will express surprise.
Still, I am unable to cry these days.

No, no, no. I haven't penned these lines. That is beyond the scope of my abilities; getting such heavy words to square up against each other and making them wrestle to draw a conclusion out of that extreme violence. This is strange in itself. Simply reading about it and listening to this makes me sweat, because for me there isn't much difference between wrestling and poetry. I still cannot fathom why people wrestle or why poetry is written. I asked Pundalik how this happens. He replied saying that wrestling is fighting from the outside, but poetry is fighting from within, with one's own self. I didn't quite understand what he said and responded with a vague 'hmmm'. Pundalik empathized with me. He said, 'Rajkumar, the problem is not that you are a novice; the problem is that you lack understanding.'

Due to all this talking, I forgot to play my game. No matter how important a task I am engrossed in, I never move ahead without playing this game of mine. I will tell you about it later. First, let me play!

Aah! Game over!

Problem . . . I am at the height of my problems. What, brother? What is the problem? This is the problem: whenever a problem surfaces, it brings along a solution, and in the wake of the solution, the problem crops up again. It is said that the one whose life has no problems has not lived a life at all. This means I have not lived life as yet, because there has never been any problem in my life. Even though I have always liked this word 'problem' and I have wanted to be surrounded by problems. There should be a mountain of problems staring at me. But I have not been fortunate enough to be blessed with any problem! Some hurdles appear, but you can't grant them the honour of being a 'problem'. But I am very happy nowadays, because it is in the form of a letter that something has come to my attention, and I can call it a problem. Today, I can speak all those sentences I have always wanted to, albeit a bit more seriously: 'Today, I . . . though I also like this word "serious" a lot. Serious . . . what a word . . . no . . . but first the problem. Today, I am facing a problem. I am sad, because today I am engulfed by a dangerous problem. What will become of me now? Am I thinking of suicide? Oh, this is the problem. Where is my knife?'

. . . Done.

Now the problem . . . no, no . . . let the problem be for now. You won't understand my problem right now. Is this even a problem, you will say. Hey, brother, to me it is a problem. But forget the problem; first things first . . . the fight. These days I am fighting. I am still fighting. So, I gather that if this fight is from within, with one's own self, then it began long ago. The actual fight began when my wisdom tooth emerged. Though, let me assert that my wisdom tooth appeared about a decade later than it usually does for average people. That's when I began to understand that I am the kind of person only a few people like; and 'few' means maybe three or four people, one of them being my mother. She is so used to getting irritated with me and scolding me by saying she cannot live without me. Whenever I do something, like perform a chore, I am prepared to face Mother's strange facial expression; those wrinkles getting deeper on that lined face and her strange ritual of raising her arms to make up for her short stature. I am used to all of that. We both like each other a lot.

I am a man of average stature, but I can appear taller by wearing slightly tight clothes and Raghu's heeled shoes. Some people say that I look quite all right when I wear Raghu's shoes and that fitted red T-shirt. I always do everything right, and everybody knows that. When my school results were declared, and if someone asked Mother about it, she would always say my result was okay. I was born okay. I grew up okay, too. Actually, I always stay at a point that is exactly equidistant between good and bad. The point that you call the midpoint on a scale, and I call okay. Once, during the selections for the school cricket team, there was a two-hour-long discussion on whether to select me or not. For the first time, I felt important. Half of the people in the discussion said I should be selected; that I didn't play poorly. The other half said I shouldn't be selected because I didn't play too well either. My stand was: 'Sir . . . Sir, I play alright.' Nobody understood. Oh! They were unable to find a word to describe how I play. When I used the word 'alright' and said that I play alright, everyone was angry with me and asked what that meant! Alright means nothing, they said. Ever since, my only association with cricket has been watching other people play. Anyone can get deluded by looking at my body. Many would even think that I cannot even run. So, I surprise everyone when I play a game—either a new one or an old one—and I play it okay. The problem begins there. I can never move beyond that point. I reach the okay point the first day itself, and then even after years of playing, I never move beyond it.

Mother tells me that I was very fat when I was young. People used to say that I ate up my father as soon as I was born, which is why I was so fat. Each time I remember this, I laugh a lot. I gobbled up my father . . . *gupp* . . . *gupp* . . . *gupp* . . . became fat, and then suddenly began to get thinner. Mother has a reason for that, too. I had once eaten a bar of Rin soap. Licked it off . . . lick . . . lick . . . and walked a short distance when I collapsed with a thud. That's when Mother realized I had fainted. She tells me she had seen the film *Mother India* just before this incident. She picked me up in her arms and ran towards the hospital. I haven't seen the film, but why did she run? Actually, my mother wanted to play the role of a mother to the hilt at least once, and she did. She ran for about one-and-a-half kilometres carrying heavy and chubby me; she was perspiring profusely. However, when she reached the hospital, the doctor scolded her. He said because of her running, the Rin soap had become foam and was oozing out from everywhere. Mother tells me that the doctor took out two mugfulls of water from me. Then he asked her to take precautions as I had become very weak. He said I had to be given extra care and attention for many years to come. And that I should not sustain any head injuries until I was ten and so on.

Perhaps my wisdom tooth got delayed because I ate a detergent bar. But how does one know when wisdom has actually arrived? Because this is not an electric bulb that comes alive at the press of a button. So how does one know? One day, Pundalik asked me this question. I suppose he wanted to test my wisdom. I was scared. I didn't think much before responding quickly, for had I not done that, he would have presumed that I had no wisdom. I said, if one feels that whatever one has done in the past was stupid, that's an indication of having attained wisdom. He laughed. I thought I had said something wrong. I added to my statement and said that the realization takes place in the molar in the corner of one's mouth. Oh! Never before had I felt so embarrassed in my life. Pundalik laughed. He laughed so much that he started perspiring profusely, and then he spat out his reply: 'By gosh! What an answer!' Each word from his mouth was like a wrestler's punch on my face: hit, hit, hit!

He kept speaking without pause for at least two hours. I cannot narrate the whole of it, so let me tell you the highlights.

> *The flower did catch your flutter.*
> *This story is yours and mine.*
> *Imagine the bumblebee came,*
> *Imagine the molar hurt,*
> *The moment I removed the hand from the tooth.*
> *My feet tapped in pain.*
> *Tap . . . tap . . . tap . . .*
> *Tap . . . tap . . . tap*
> *Tap . . . tap . . . tap . . .*
> *Tap . . . tap . . . tap*
> *But your heart*
> *Sitting on my cycle's tyre*
> *Tyre puncture, wisdom is the king*
> *Whenever the brain in the knee worked*

Made a whirring noise like a fan
Kharr . . . kharr . . . kharr
The weight of the earth
Grandchild of the frog
A drop of dew
Elephant's tusk
Wisdom tooth
Bite in the mouth
Night moon
Morning sun
The moment it rose
All the sparrows
Pharr . . . pharr . . . pharr . . .
Pharr . . . pharr . . . pharr . . .

That day nothing registered with me: when did Pundalik rise and leave? When did the night fall? When did the day dawn . . .? There was only one purpose to my life now; that I should say something that would amaze Pundalik. I wanted to see beads of perspiration on his forehead.

Pundalik was a strange man: he never celebrated his birthday. He used to say that he was not born; he had simply appeared. For me, he had indeed just appeared. He was my mother's brother and had come to live in our house one fine day. I couldn't believe it. You see, I have known my mother for years. Could there be others who were my mother's own other than me? I don't know! He used to call himself a great poet and me a great listener, because I was just lonely. I was very happy when he recited his first poem to me. Since then, I didn't know about him, but my greatness kept growing. But our relationship of a poet and listener was somewhat reversed. After reciting each poem, Pundalik would begin to praise me, because he loved the look of amazement on my face. I was as such bereft of expressions. But this was one expression I could successfully express to Pundalik. Because I could not comprehend ninety out of the hundred things he said, and whatever little I did, I would be scared of saying it.

Pundalik had cried in front of me several times. He harboured a great sadness; I don't exactly know what it was, but there was definitely something. But whenever he cried in front of me, I used to feel like laughing. I would get the sense that Pundalik was ashamed of his crying. He would suppress his crying in a strange way. He would stiffen his whole body in a strange posture, contort his face like a monkey, and produce a strange sharp noise . . . eee . . . eee . . . eee. He loved his mother a lot. He used to say that he had lived with her till her very last day. Maybe my mother didn't like her mother as much. I don't know, but Pundalik had told me so. Loving your mother . . . I haven't understood till date what it is like to love your mother. Whenever I look at my mother, she seems like a piece of dry wood. Someone who keeps scouting, very quietly, for more work around the house. Isn't it strange, that we have been living together in the same house for years? I sometimes feel that the house is not a house but a boat which has holes in it at various places. My mother sits right in the middle of that boat with a mug, and with that mug, she continuously throws out the water that seeps in.

Talking of my mother reminds me I should play my game right now.

It becomes imperative for me to play my favourite game when I reach someplace else in my thoughts. My game first, everything else later!

Aah! Game over!

* * *

Pundalik used to teasingly say that my mother was very lazy. Oh! Why did he say that? He always said something of this nature just before he left, and I keep thinking about it. Gradually, it dawned on me that other than the *Mother India* incident, my mother is actually lazy. This can be proven by the simple act of how she named me. Well, you see, she named me Raju, which is the name of every second person in India. And while getting me admitted to school, she extended her affection by making it Rajkumar. Mother tells me that while filling the admission form, the school clerk was laughing as he looked at me. She felt it was because of my odd face. I do feel that every person must have the option to choose their own name.

As a matter of fact, my mother was very mysterious. Nobody else knows this except me. Whenever she took out her red ribbon from the cupboard, it was to be understood that she was dressing up to go out. She loved watching films alone. And not any religious films; instead, she preferred films full of romance and action. I don't know about romance, but action had a huge impact on her. As she aged, her face grew more and more masculine. She had even begun to sprout a beard and a moustache, and at every instance she would scold me saying, 'You dog! I will drink your blood!'

Around that time, Pundalik gave me a book: Maxim Gorky's *Mother*. I was surprised. Until then I used to believe that all mothers behaved in the same manner, as part of some secret society. But what was this! Pundalik told me that it was a true story. I wondered how mothers could be so! I remembered that Pundalik had told me that he loved his mother a lot. And so, I wanted to know more about his mother. I asked: 'Pundalik, is your mother also like Gorky's mother?' It seemed like there was a volcano inside Pundalik that was triggered as soon as it came in contact with my question. He started to talk and didn't stop. He used such words and examples that I found the story quite engrossing. But I didn't understand much, and hence, I used my ultimate weapon—the expression of amazement. Observing that expression he slowed down a little, and in his heavy voice began to speak slowly so that I could comprehend what he was saying. He said: 'During Mother's last days, I had stopped reading, writing or going out of the house. I simply stayed with her all the time. I used to recite the Gita to her. I didn't leave the house for years. She passed away listening to the Gita. She died all of a sudden. I felt strange and empty. I couldn't understand anything. Just then, her smiling face began to hover in front of my eyes, and it turned into a tree; I sat under the tree and began to write.

Sunshine is burning the face
The shadow is eating up the shoe
The body is dispelling water
A tree is coming closer
In her cloak I've been raised
Drinking the breath of her affection
I am still full of life
You won't believe
But in this forest a tree has watered me
I call her Mother
When night has gobbled up the noise
When our anxiety makes sleep shorter than the night
When our cowardice interferes in our dreams
Then her fingers move on my forehead
And I sleep.

And he slept. I sat stunned. Good that he slept, because I didn't want to cry in front of him. I ran out of his room and saw her. I saw the woman who looked like dry wood and whose face was becoming masculine; the one who had thrown out mugfulls of water. I began to shiver from head to toe. I felt as if I had seen my mother for the first time. I ran and embraced her, and uttered: Pelagaya Nilobana, my mother.

Smack! I heard some noise. My head began to whirl. For many days I could feel her fingers full of maternal love on my cheek. But I was not disheartened by this incident. I didn't stop calling her Mother. Though the fact is that I would, in my heart, say Mother, and call out to her as Maa.

Mother, and then Maa . . . like that. The dialogues exchanged between my mother and me had been fixed years ago. No incident had any bearing on those dialogues whatsoever.

Pundalik had once said that there was no difference between my village and me. He said this and simply walked off. I didn't understand what he meant. I kept thinking, and after a long while I understood that it was true. Actually, my village was not a village, but it was not a city either. The people here were not very rich but they were not starving. It was not important enough to be mentioned in a map of the country and not so insignificant that it was like it did not exist at all. The inhabitants of the village did not want to do anything but in the end everyone ended up doing something or the other. Everything here worked okay, just like me! Pundalik says that this village seems to be inhabited by people who somehow got left behind. Like a truck full of sand leaves some of it behind; similarly, some people who were left behind got together and constituted this village.

My village was equidistant from the highway and the jungle. But my house was at the edge of the highway. Across the road was a dhaba where strange-faced people would make loud noises while having food. It seemed as if the voices of those people had become voices of their vehicles. I rarely went to the other side of the road during the day, though. I went at about five in the morning and I would write something behind a truck. I knew that these trucks traversed the whole country—many villages, towns and cities. I would write something with chalk in small letters behind the trucks. I do not know for whom. But it was like sending a message to the universe. I strongly believed that somewhere some Raju, Rajkumar, Chhotu, Bunty, Chintu, Rakesh . . . some ordinary person with an ordinary name like me would wake up at 5 a.m. and read my message. Because all that I wrote never came back to me. So, it meant that there was someone who read what I wrote and then erased it so that no one else could read it. This friendship had progressed a lot. I would convey all my thoughts to my mysterious friend, albeit briefly. I would beat around the bush cleverly so that no one else could laugh at my thoughts. What if the police found out and reached my home! Because I had written the secrets of everyone there—Raghu's, Mother's, Pundalik's and Radhey's—everyone's secrets. But I was smart, and the police would not be able to figure out anything. Because long ago I had informed my truck-friend that from now on Pundalik = poet, Raghu = hero, Radhey = Gandhi's stick, Mother = woman with the mug.

There were two objectives behind waking up at 5 a.m. While the first was to scribble my message on the truck, the second was to meet Radhey. Radhey would arrive in front of my house every morning at 5 a.m. I do not actually know whether his name was Radhey or not. Whenever he met me, he said Radhey-Radhey and I said Radhey-Radhey back to him. We were both Radhey for each other. I used to call him the old man who has gold, because he was a gold-digger. Actually, there were two small gold and silver shops in our home, from which we received rent. Radhey would come every morning with his iron-toothed broom and try to collect gold flecks. While collecting them, he would become like a white bundle that would constantly roll in front of my eyes. He would remain absolutely quiet while working. I could only hear his breathing.

I had known Radhey for many years now. It seemed like he was stuck at a particular age. And perhaps it was not possible for him to ever age further. He was the same old and aged person for many years now. It seemed impossible that Radhey could ever have been a child. He had left the village to visit the outside world just once; that was his first and last journey. He had gone all the way to Sabarmati Ashram, to see Gandhiji. This was his only achievement in life, and I had heard about it at least fifty times by now. Every time he would narrate the incident, the sequence of events leading to his meeting Gandhiji was different. Just like him, Gandhiji said a different thing each time. Sometimes, Gandhiji would have simply said a polite 'Namaste', and Radhey had come back. At other times, Radhey had a meal with Gandhiji. On other occasions, Gandhiji had wanted to say something to him, but Radhey was in a hurry to come back to the village. Once, Gandhiji had even said to Radhey that he was very tired, and that Radhey should now become Gandhi.

While he picked gold, I would speak very little with him. Once, however, I did ask him why he picked gold. He replied saying that it was his wish to visit the Vaishno Devi shrine before he died. I asked how much money he needed to go to Vaishno Devi. He said at least Rs 1000. Don't you have that much, I asked. I have it, Radhey said.

What kind of a thing was that! I found it very strange. I asked him that if he wanted to visit the deity's shrine and if he also had the money for it, then why didn't he go? Radhey went silent. It was a strange silence, and I didn't deem it wise to intervene. Radhey then slowly said: 'A few days after I met Gandhiji, he died. I was very sad. His stone statue was installed at the Gandhi Park in our village. It seemed as if Gandhiji had left instructions before dying that his idol must be put in Radhey's village. I would stand in front of that statue for hours. Gandhiji, too, kept looking at me for hours. It seemed as if he wanted to say something to me. But because the park was very crowded, he wasn't able to. Then, one day, he appeared in my dream. In fact, he summoned me to his ashram. I saw him there with a large crowd. He looked at me and called out my name. I greeted him. He embraced me and softly told me to go to Vaishno Devi. I was surprised at this. When I looked towards Gandhiji, he had transformed into a dove and was flying away. That's when I suddenly woke up. As soon as it was morning, I went to meet Gandhiji at the Gandhi Park and what do I see! That same dove was sitting on his head there. The dream was true, absolutely true! Until then, I had only left the village once to step into the world outside, so I was very scared. I tried to, but couldn't go then; now, I don't even want to. Because I have lived my whole life in this hope of visiting the Vaishno Devi shrine someday. So, if I do go, how will I spend the rest of my days? I have nurtured this hope in which I have lived to such an extent that it has grown like my son. Now, at this age, I cannot murder my son.'

Murder reminded me that I hadn't played my game for some time now. I will quickly play it and come right back!

Aah! Game over!

I remember I had read about Gandhiji in my school. Our Ma-saheb (Master Saheb)—in the village, the teacher is called Ma-saheb—would teach us about Gandhiji in a disinterested manner. Neither would Ma-saheb like telling us nor would we like listening about Gandhiji. I did not like it at all, because by then I had entered the grand and shiny world of Raghu.

Raghu . . . Raghu . . . Raghu . . . he was a miracle. He was very good-looking. Everybody was scared of him because his father was in the police and had been transferred to our village and, also, because in the entire village only he could speak a little bit of English. Even our school Ma-saheb was scared of him because our Hindi-speaking teachers were no match for his English. For me, from Class IX to XI, Raghu was like Krishna and people like me were the cows who danced to the tunes of his flute. He was an eclectic mix of a deer, a lion and a horse. He would always be late for class. And the sound of his arrival entered the class before he did, like a horse . . . gallop . . . gallop . . . gallop. The moment he appeared at the door of the class, intimidated by his lion's mane-like hair, Ma-saheb would leave his seat.

Raghu wore heeled shoes and tight clothes. He was very different. Raghu was a class apart from the entire village. What's more, he didn't believe in any Indian God; rather, a foreign God whose pictures he had pasted all over his house. He would keep repeating that he was God! Once he told me that his God was so swift that when it was time to sleep and he turned off the light, his God was asleep even before the bulb stopped glowing. Once, I sheepishly asked Raghu: 'Raghu, which religion does your God manage?' He laughed. After laughing for a long time, he said something in English which I did not comprehend. Our relationship was similar to that of Krishna and his cow. We had never spoken directly with each other; I could never gather the courage to do so. I had written a lot to my truck-friend about Raghu. The time that I was fascinated with Raghu—I would chase and stalk him through the day—I only went home to sleep. I had forgotten about eating and drinking.

He had a strange but beautiful red cycle. When he would ride it wearing his heeled shoes and tight red T-shirt, he looked simply amazing! I would run behind the cycle to hear its bell. When Raghu parked it to go somewhere, I would sneak up and gently ring that bell. What a sound it made! Not like our village bicycles that have a shrill and crude sound . . . *tan* . . . *tan*. His bell would go *tring* . . . *tring*. But one day, he came to school and announced that he was leaving the village. I began to cry instantly. I stood up in class and almost shouted, 'No, Raghu; no, you cannot leave me and go. How can you do this to me? No! No!' When I fell quiet, I heard the whole class laughing. I could not bear it. I got up and left the class. While leaving, I wanted to see Raghu's face once. Was he, too, laughing at me? But I couldn't gather the courage to look at him. I was embarrassed by my own behaviour. When I woke up the following morning, I embraced Radhey and cried a lot. He tried to placate me by saying, 'Doesn't matter. These things happen. Don't cry. When I was parting ways with Gandhiji, he, too, couldn't bear it. His eyes were brimming with tears.' This meant Radhey didn't get what I was trying to say. That was the first time I got annoyed with him and went to the other side of the road and stood by a truck for hours.

I dropped out of school. After a few days, a constable came home. He asked my mother if I was home. My instant reaction was that my scribbling behind trucks had been discovered. Now everyone would know what I thought of them. It was not the thought of being in prison that scared me. That everyone would know what I thought of them upset me! It was like being nude in public. I was petrified of the constable. I told him that I was Rajkumar, at which he laughed. He gave me a bag and said, 'While he was leaving, Raghu saheb asked me to give this to you. Namaste!' Saying this, the constable left. I opened the bag and what did I see! It had Raghu's heeled shoes and a picture of his God. How I wish you could see the picture of this strange God. Later, someone told me that Raghu's God was called Bruce Lee. Oh! God Bruce Lee! Help me! I bow before you!

I couldn't wear Raghu's shoes very often because they gave me shoe bites. But I did not stop wearing them until my feet were badly swollen. One day, Pundalik saw my swollen feet. I assumed he would be sad and would ask me what had happened. But he did no such thing. Instead, he looked at my feet, smiled, and then turned around to look towards the window. Then he slowly turned towards me, smiled, and said: 'When the shoe bites, it becomes difficult to live. And when the shoe stops biting, it becomes difficult to pass the time.'

That day, for the first time, I experienced loneliness.
I lived alone. I couldn't remember a time when someone
listened to me when I spoke. Though it is a different matter
that I had nothing much to say. But Pundalik never stayed
with me. It was I who always stayed with him. Radhey's
Gandhi narrative hadn't ended as yet. I chose to remain
silent there as well. Mother's boat was still not empty of
water. It was only my truck-friend with whom I shared
everything. However, for the first time, I doubted whether
he, wherever he was, was actually reading my messages.

The shoes remained in a corner of the house for
many days. They never became a part of the house. Later,
however, the house made them a part of it, and this noble
gesture was performed by Mother. She turned the two
long-heeled shoes into flowerpots. I saw that and even
though I felt bad, I said nothing. Because the conversations
between Mother and me had been pre-determined. I did
not want to break or change them. But they were Raghu's
shoes; my Raghu's shoes!

I badly need my game at this moment.

You must be wondering what this game is that I
keep playing again and again. Honestly, it is an amazing
game that came to me one fine day. Believe me, just like
Pundalik did! One day, sitting at home, I suddenly saw a
train. A train of ants was walking in a queue, in perfect
rhythm. I kept following them. I couldn't make out where
they had come from or where they were headed. They were
all walking in a line. I brought five grains of sugar, and the
game began. I shut the door of the house and shut out the
entire outside world. As a result, I began to see the inside

more clearly. I placed the grains of sugar parallel to the line of ants: the first two grains close by, the third slightly away, the fourth further away and the fifth right at the end. Two or three ants tried to move towards these grains. The train had turned. The moment the ants reached the fifth grain, I picked the first two and put them in front of the fifth grain. This way, I could turn that ant-train towards any direction. It was so much fun that there was someone who followed my instructions; that, too, just for five grains of sugar. This was my favourite game that I played every day.

Aah! Game over!

Ever since Pundalik had moved in with us, he rarely went anywhere. Once in a while, he would go to the city to meet his friend Tarachand Jaiswal and come back in a day. I could not play my ant game in front of him. I had never gone out of the village because Radhey had told me that it was a very dangerous world outside the village—food, language, people, everything changed. There were two cities on either side of our village and the crowds from there kept running amok on the roads of our village. When Pundalik spoke to me, it felt as if, even though he addressed me by my name, Raju, he was actually talking to himself. Because sometimes, I would simply get up and leave and when I would return, he would still be addressing 'Raju' non-stop. He was the victim of a strange loneliness. I have not presumed this; I have heard him say this to himself. Once he was reading aloud a strange text to himself: 'A dog tries to bite his own tail. Then begins a dog cyclone that only ends when the dog escapes this storm as a dog. Loneliness—this dog and I look into each other's eyes.'

Pundalik told me that he was an established poet. He had tried to write all kinds of poems—romantic poems, intense poems about pain, on children, about the environment, about rocks, about flowers . . . but no one had paid any heed. People would see him approach and start to run away. Pundalik would shout: 'No, brother, now I will not recite any poem.' But no one would stop. If someone did, Pundalik would end up reciting a poem to them by hook or by crook. Pundalik says that people had begun to make fun of him. Whichever house he entered; one could hear a lot of noise from within that house. Pundalik had also written poems about children and so children had stopped playing in the locality. Every child was scared of the name Pundalik. People would deliver vegetables and groceries to his house because no one wanted to hear any poem by Pundalik under any circumstances. Publishing them was too far-fetched an expectation. Nowadays, after reciting his poems, Pundalik would not praise me. Instead, he would get angry. Once, after reciting a poem, he asked, 'Why, you didn't like the poem?' I said, 'No, it was good.' He said, 'Then why are you looking at me with anger?' Oh! This was strange! He himself had told me that he wanted to turn me into a serious listener. You already know how much I love this word . . . serious! Serious, what a word! But, brother, when a serious expression comes over another expression that expresses amazement, your face appears distorted in a strange way. What do I do! I had tried my best to be a serious listener.

Distortion reminded me that, one day, a strange thing occurred. I was playing my ant game when I felt I myself had become an ant. What? I began to feel strange. I felt as if playing that game my intellect had also been reduced to that of an ant! Just then, I saw the grains of sugar. And what do I see—that those grains of sugar, instead of grains, have become Raghu, Pundalik, Radhey, my mother and my truck-friend. And I had begun to run ahead of them. This means that there is someone who is playing with me, while I am not playing. The way that I play with the ants, the ants don't play with me. Who knows! Maybe the ants are also playing with someone who isn't playing with the ants. This means everyone is playing with everyone. This means Pundalik is also playing with me.

Now you probably understand my problem. I have a huge problem because of which I am doing all of this. This problem came to me in the form of Pundalik. Actually, Pundalik wanted to get his poetry collection published. His friend in the city, Tarachand Jaiswal, was helping him get his anthology published. I had already listened to all his poems, to some of them so many times that I had even memorized them. The problem began when Pundalik was leaving home one day. While leaving, I saw that he was carrying with him the diary in which he wrote down his poetry, a letter, my mother's photograph and the Gita. He brought all of this to me. He asked me to put both my hands on them and swear . . . swear, by your mother, by the Gita, by my poems that you will surely get my poetry anthology published. Before I could swear and promise, I noticed that he had already packed his stuff. I asked, 'Where are you going, Pundalik?' The city was not very far from our village; I mean, he didn't need to pack to go there. He did not answer my question. His voice sounded strange. He kept insisting that I must swear and so I did. I swore by the goddess of learning, the mother earth, the poems, the Gita, and I added two or three more from my side. It didn't matter much to me!

The poetry anthology was Pundalik's and Tarachand Jaiswal was going to publish it. Who was I in the whole scenario? Actually, I was nobody and that's why I could not understand why Pundalik insisted that I swear that I would get his poetry anthology published! Honestly, by swearing, I had been caught in his trap. As soon as the swearing ritual was complete, Pundalik's face brightened up. He threw Mother's photo and the Gita aside, picked up his stuff, and left. As he reached the door, he realized that I had asked him where he was going. He turned around and said, 'First, I am going to the city to give Tarachand Jaiswal these poems and this letter in which I have written everything about you and the poems. After that I am going on a pilgrimage and then I am going to live my life as an ascetic.' He said this and embraced me, and said softly in my ear, 'I wanted to give you something. You will get it after I leave. Thank you. Namaste.' And he left!

It was all right to write about his poems, but why had he written about me in the letter? What did he want to give me, and why? I had only listened to his poems, and I didn't understand half of them. If there was a mention of any listener in the letter, I wouldn't have objected. However, that was not the case. I was badly stuck. How Pundalik had trapped me in this problem became clear from a letter that I received from Tarachand Jaiswal a few days after he had left.

I mean, how could Pundalik do this to me! I couldn't believe it! I know that I am not a very useful man, but that someone could use me like this! I could not believe it at all! You know what he did! What was written in Tarachand Jaiswal's letter? This is his letter. Since the letter is very long, I will only tell you the main points:

Rajkumar,
My greetings to the great poet! I was delighted to read your poems. Pundalik had mentioned about your poems earlier as well. Everyone here is praising your work. The anthology will be published by next month, but there is a problem. The anthology is short by one poem. This is not my opinion, but our editor's. You are a renowned poet. After the publication of this collection, you will find your name being mentioned alongside the all-time great poets. Kindly send one more poem at the earliest. My daughter, too, is a huge fan of your poetry. What is your view about getting married? Pundalik used to praise you a lot. When can we meet? In the collection . . . would you like your name to be simply Rajkumar or would you like to add a pseudonym, too? Do let me know.
Yours,
Tarachand Jaiswal

So, now, the problem had become dangerously gigantic. Why did I swear? Now I regret it. Forget about my promise.

I do want Pundalik's poetry anthology to be published, but like this? No!

I searched in Pundalik's books for several days, just in case he had written down four lines, two lines, even a single line of a poem somewhere. But I found nothing. Then I picked up a pen and began to write, trying to think like Pundalik.

I couldn't. Actually, nothing much has happened in my life that can be written about. I do remember everything that has happened, but believe me, it is as good as if it never happened. As Pundalik used to say, it is imperative for writing poems that boys like him go through experiences. When they face those experiences, whatever they write becomes poetry. Wow! Neither did I understand this back then nor do I get it now. I mean, I can understand wrestling. But poetry is still a surprise for me. What fight? To fight with whom? The search within? This was beyond me back then and it is still beyond me. But I have no other option. I need to do this now. And it is not as if I have not started writing. Since the last four days, I have already written the beginning and end of the letter I will send to Tarachand Jaiswal. The beginning reads thus:

Namaskar Tarachand Jaiswalji,
Namaste! How are you? I am fine. You must be fine.
My poem is as follows:
(The part that should have the poem is a blank space at present.)
This is the end.

The above written poem is fine. I am also fine. Sorry
for the inconvenience. After sending this poem, I
am leaving this house, this village, this city and this
country. Don't try to follow me. Please publish the
poetry anthology. Promise me.
Your obedient poet,
Rajkumar 'Gambhir'.

I had adopted 'Gambhir' (Serious) as my pseudonym.
Though I also like the word problem, the name 'Rajkumar
Serious Problem' doesn't seem to be a good idea.

This part is done, but how do I write the poem? I have
to write it. All the roads are closed. It's a long, straight
road. There is not even a lane, by-lane, pathway to take
a detour and hide. So, I have to move forward and write.
Had I sworn upon only one thing, I swear I would have
broken the promise. But all the promises I had made in
enthusiasm had now turned into ghosts and were chasing
me. Oh Gandhiji, please save me. Oh God, please save me.
No, no, I can't be saved by them. Only a poet can save a
poet. Now only Pundalik can save me. He had said fight
with your own self and so I am fighting.

* * *

When Pundalik had told me about his mother and how he
had cared for her during her last days, I began to imagine
the things that I would do for my mother in her last days.
First of all, I decided I would snatch away the mug from her
hand and throw it far away. And for once, I myself would

make her wear the red ribbon and take her to the cinema. Because I really wished to see how Mother watched a film. How did she stand in the queue for the tickets? What did she do in the interval, and what was the connection between her red ribbon and watching a film? But all of these wishes of mine remained mere wishes. Because one morning, I woke up and realized Mother was not in her bed. She was lying fallen on the floor, face down, near the door. And the red ribbon was in her hair. I cried out, 'Maa! Maa!' Then I even said 'Mother', but she didn't stir.

I was scared. I went to wake up Pundalik, but before that I removed the red ribbon from her hair and kept it in my pocket. I didn't want anyone else to know about her watching films. Pundalik came out. He announced that I should make arrangements; that my mother was dead. How did this happen! What arrangements is he talking about, and how is this possible! I wasn't in grief but in shock, because I wasn't worried about myself, but about the house. Will this house say nothing? Mother didn't live with us, she lived with the house. Maybe this house should have died first. Maybe that's why Mother had not died in her bed but on the floor—in the lap of this house. Pundalik asked me to make preparations, and he went away, leaving me alone with Mother. What could I do? I turned her over. I kept a pillow under her head and started watching her stiff, wooden body. This had given birth to me. It seemed strange! Pundalik brought things for the cremation, and a few people also came along. Even though I wasn't crying, yet everyone was telling me not to worry; that this was life, and everything would be all right, and so on. Then they shaved my head, and I lit her pyre. I watched my mother's body burn. Suddenly, I saw her hand in between all the wood. It felt as if she was asking for her mug. I wanted to bring her mug and make her hold it, or at least take out the red ribbon from my pocket and throw it in the burning pyre. But I couldn't garner enough courage. I quietly watched her body burn. My mother lay between the burning planks of wood. As I was returning home, my thoughts went to the house. Would it have vanished? It must have fallen or there must be at least a deep crack somewhere. But there was nothing of the sort. Everything was normal.

> When sunshine burns the face,
> The shadow takes a back seat,
> The body is getting rid of water
> And a tree is closing in,
> I have been raised in her lap
> Drinking in the breath of her affection,
> I am still flourishing
> You won't believe
> But a tree has nurtured me in this jungle
> I call it Mother.

* * *

Radhey was quite sad these days. He spent a lot of time in Gandhi Park, with Gandhiji. He would say that, nowadays, he and Gandhiji talked a lot. That Gandhiji heard him out and had even forgiven him. That Gandhiji sometimes became adamant about visiting Vaishno Devi. But he was sad because, in this village, it was the time of the year to go to Vaishno Devi. Some people were on their way to the shrine, some were returning from there; but they all chased Radhey away. He had suddenly stopped coming over. A lot of dust had accumulated in front of the house. Since Radhey wasn't skimming through it, I felt a lot of gold must be present in it. I swept and collected all the dust, keeping it safe for Radhey. I thought he would be very happy, but he didn't show up. Suddenly, he appeared one day. I asked, 'Radhey, where have you been for so many days?' He didn't say anything but sat quietly. I continued, 'I even went to Gandhi Park to look for you, but you weren't there either.' He still stayed quiet. Maybe he didn't want to reply. So I, too, remained seated quietly. Radhey even refused to take all the dust I had collected for him. He said it was of no use to him anymore. Saying this, he turned into a white bundle and began to roll in front of me. For the first time, I had experienced someone's absence from my life so intensely: Radhey's. Though Pundalik had also gone away and Mother, too, was no more, I had never felt their absence. Until Radhey hadn't come by, I was fighting with the empty space within me; so much so that I could even hear my own voice echoing.

This is it. This is the only significant thing that has happened in my life; nothing else is worth mentioning. There are a few other minor things—like a dog had started coming to meet me behind the house every day. I, too, had begun to spend time with him in the evenings. But just as I had started thinking about giving him a name, he stopped coming.

Now, it's just Radhey, my truck-friend and me. Only the three of us remain and we are happy. All the fighting is over. This is all that I can remember. But I don't consider it worthy enough to write poetry about. Pundalik is a poet, not poetry. My mother is also just my mother. She is not like Gorky's or Pundalik's mother. There are incidents about my mother; there is no poetry. Radhey is Radhey. He is the stick in the hands of the statue of Gandhiji in Gandhi Park, nothing more than that. I prefer to remain silent about my truck-friend. Raghu was, is, and shall remain a miracle for me. He is my Raghu. But poetry he is not! I fought with my inner self as much as I could. Where is the poem hidden! I have sworn upon so many things. What will happen to all those promises? Tarachand Jaiswal is waiting there. I have not been able to write even a single word here. Pundalik, forgive me. I won't be able to do it. Let all the promises go to hell! No, no. None of this will work. I am doing all this to distract myself. I am playing a game with myself. This won't last for very long. I have to write, and I will write now.

. . . I wrote. Now whatever it is that I have written, please accept it. Oh Tarachand Jaiswalji, here is your letter, finally complete! Now you may make of it whatever you will. I shall read the whole letter to you. So here is the beginning:

Namastey Tarachand ji,
Namastey! How are you? I hope you are good. My
poem is as follows:
(In the middle, this poem)

Five grains of sugar are the magic
That the ants chase
They reach two grains
And see three ahead and call all the other ants.
They reach the fifth grain and forget the two grains
behind them,
Then the same two grains are found ahead. They get
trapped in the magic.
And keep roaming. This game never ends.
Because the ants are on a quest and aren't playing a game.
The magician is the one playing the game.

And now this is the end, in the end:

The above written poem is okay. I am also okay.
Forgive me. After sending this poem I will be going
away from this house, this village, this city and
this country. Don't try to follow me. Promise me you
will surely publish the poetry anthology.
Yours obediently
Poet Rajkumar 'Gambhir'

Is it okay? It is okay!

Now that this has ended, I can now play my game in a
relaxed manner. Where are my ants, and where are my five
grains of sugar?

Words and Their Pictures

I wanted to write her name. Instead, I wrote 'Asha'. Then I began to look for her. Her picture was etched within 'Asha' itself. 'Asha,' I said softly. No, I didn't actually say it; I just read what I had written.

I could see her approaching from a distance. She was wearing something brown. As she came closer, huge sunflowers were visible on the brown. While some were blooming, some had withered away. The whole landscape was dull and pale. Her arrival seemed like an escape from something else. She wasn't walking but running. She wanted to fly but was entangled somewhere on the ground. Then I uttered the word 'butterfly', and she came even closer.

'Where had you gone?' I asked.

'To look for water,' she said, wiping beads of perspiration.

'Water?'

'Yes, water.'

'So where is the water?'

'I drank it,' she said nonchalantly, and walked away.

I didn't know whether she knew that I had been waiting for her. I began to follow her. After walking for a while, I uttered another word: 'soft'. She stopped walking. I did not have the courage to say, 'I, too, am thirsty.' Instead, I asked: 'Where are you going?'

'Further towards the hills.'

I could see the end of the desert, beyond which lay the sprawled expanse of the hills.

'So why didn't you come looking for water this side?'

'This is a different direction.'

'Yes, but if you had to come this side anyway, shouldn't you have walked towards here!'

'This is a different direction.'

I had never changed my direction. I knew only one direction in which I had to move. I took along with me all those who I met on that path. How can thirst and water have different directions? Why should they be different? I could never understand the relationship between the desert and the path to thirst.

She was standing quietly in front of me. Maybe she could read the conflict in my mind. I was thirsty. My throat was parched. If I spoke, my questions were likely to be sharp. But I remained quiet. She was expecting me to speak; I could read that in her eyes. Since I wasn't sure if I could question, I merely said, 'Hills.' We had reached a spot somewhere near Mukhteshwar. She was climbing one mountain after another looking for someone. I was left behind. When my breathlessness began to disturb the peace of the mountains, she sat under a cedar. I almost crawled up to her and then lay sprawled beside her. She laughed. No, this wasn't her laughter; it was the laughter of the mountains. Maybe the cedars were laughing. I turned around and looked at her. There was no laughter on her lips, but I could still hear it. In response to my surprise, she said, 'Voices echo in the hills. Whatever you say keeps coming back to you.' I noticed that she had applied kaajal. I could see tiny peals of laughter in the black of the kaajal. I now uttered the word 'playful'.

She was instantly reminded of something. She told me that somewhere here near the hills was her school. A tree plantation programme had once been organized in the school. All the children had to plant trees, and by the time it was her turn there were no more saplings left. After looking around for a long time, she found a small cedar sapling lying in a corner. She kept searching for a spot to plant it. The school compound was full of saplings and there was no more space left for that cedar. Her teacher told her that a cedar grows very slowly. It will take about fifteen–twenty years to grow as big as you, the teacher had said. She said that she finds this fact about cedars very beautiful . . . that they take their own sweet time to grow. When she didn't find any space in the school compound, she began to walk towards her home carrying the young cedar. In the middle of the forest, on an edge, she saw some space. There was no tree there, and so she planted the sapling.

Maybe she had come to look for her cedar.

She said, 'I feel cedars are like fathers. I become a child again sitting near them . . . my heart no longer complains about anything.'

'Yes, you had told me this.'

'When?'

'When we were having tea sitting by your blue window and the breeze was playing games with the yellow curtains of the window.'

'I don't recall this at all.'

She is right. She doesn't remember because this never happened. We've never had tea by the blue window and the yellow curtains. Though I have always wanted to sit with her at leisure, by a blue window and yellow curtains. My cedar is blue, and it has yellow leaves, sitting under which I become a child, without any complaints.

Neither of us desired anything anymore. The cedar under which we were sitting—she had presumed it to be hers and I, mine. She was picking on the past sitting there. Yes, that's what she was doing. At regular intervals, she would attack my back with her beak. I was thinking about those impermanent colours, collecting which was now my hobby. Readymade permanent colours bored me. I was sitting close to her and yet there was some space between us. And I experienced, for the first time, God, in between her attacks and my impermanent colours.

'There is a hole in your back,' she said, pecking at me once more with her beak.

'The tradition of making nests runs in my blood,' I said to her. She was ready for her next hit when I said another word: 'God'.

And we set out on a journey.

We were standing by the door of the general compartment of a crowded train. Whenever someone used the toilets, a strong stench would fill the whole compartment. She would shrink, twist her face and cover her nose with her kerchief. She gradually came closer to me. She was holding my sweater at the waist. I was watching the scenery running by. Perhaps she was tired.

'How far is it?'

'There is still time.'

There was still a lot of distance to be covered. Some people offered her a seat but she declined. The train was halting at stations, and we were getting off the train at almost every station. She would immediately sit on a bench after disembarking. Fatigue seemed to be flowing from her body. The train halted for more than its scheduled time at this particular station.

'Which station is this?' she asked, surprised. 'The board says Budhni. Have you come here before?'

'No, I am even hearing the name for the first time. And you?'

'I have heard the name . . . there is a forest here, maybe the forests of Satpura, about which Bhawani bhai has also written a poem.'

'Do you know Bhawani bhai?'

'He is a poet, and I have read his work. So, in a way I know him.'

'You added "bhai" to his name as if you have been associated with him for years.'

'How do you like the name Budhni?'

'It's a strange name.'

'Don't you find the name mysterious?'

'Maybe it is close to the forests, and so . . .'

'Do you think you will ever visit this place?'

'I don't know. There are so many places where I will never be able to go.'

'The train will move on in a while. We would have left Budhni far behind. Perhaps its mystery could be jumped into. Maybe we could jump into the mystery together.'

Just then, she said a word: 'hopefully'.

And we both began to walk barefoot on the tendu leaves in the forests of Budhni. In the distance, a temple was visible on top of a hill. We started walking towards it.

'Why did you lie to me?' she asked.

'About what?'

I was suddenly cautious.

'About the blue window and the yellow curtains.'

'Oh! That blue window and yellow curtains are the image of the word "hopefully".'

'"Hopefully", I was somewhere between the curtains and the window?'

'No, you were not between them.'

'So where was I?'

'You were inside, in the room. I wasn't there. I was standing below, on the road, and looking up at the window of your room on the third floor. The blue window and yellow curtains were swaying with the wind.'

'When did this happen?'

'This is in the future . . . a future I have imagined.'

'What happens in that future?'

'It is the imaginary world of our last meeting. Let me narrate it like a story, right from the beginning.'

We had walked right up to the hilltop and had reached the small temple that we had seen from below. There was no one in that temple. A small Shiva idol was placed there. She covered her head with her dupatta and bowed in front of it. I sat leaning against the wall of the temple, and after finishing her ritual, she came and sat by my side.

'Yes, now tell me the story.'

I uttered the word 'pain', and she began to feel pain. I started the tale right at the beginning, as if I was reading a story and not narrating it.

* * *

Each time he crossed a crowded market, he would become withdrawn. In such moments, he thought about love, relationships and women, especially the ones for whom he had gotten over the pain of 'this-relationship-could-have-been-saved'. What remained now were the hazy memories and the tingling of the beautiful moments spent with them. He would often smile thinking about those relationships. Right after the smile would emerge the pain. Everything about those relationships had become so distant that even the pain associated with them had lost its meaning. But this pain was related to those relationships that had not yet come to a closure. At such times, he would stop and want to have tea.

He had a strange relationship with tea. When he was born, he was very fair. Everyone at home felt that this was a special thing that the family had been blessed with. So, everyone would take special care of that special thing.

He developed the habit of drinking tea from childhood, the reason being that tea was not available to him. His father loved to have tea. After pleading and crying for many days, his father allowed him one cup of tea at 4 p.m. every day.

The moment he would wake up in the morning, he would begin to wait for 4 p.m. He would be served tea exactly at that time. And the moment he had the last sip, he would start waiting for the next day's tea.

He sat at a tea stall.

'Give me a strong chai.'

He really liked this whole ritual, right from the ordering of the tea to the moment tea was served to him. He loved the process more than the actual act of drinking tea.

Someone loving you . . . your being loved . . . it is such a beautiful state of being, even if it is only for a few moments. He was almost unconscious at such moments, thinking about the pain caused by relationships. In those moments, he wanted to beg and plead that there was nothing special about him.

Right then the memory of a person with whom he had shared several such lonely moments came to him. This was one woman for whom the warmth of 'this-relationship-could-have-been-saved' had still not left him.

He began to walk home from the tea stall. After covering a small distance, he turned left instead of walking towards his home. This turn was like a wound within. It hurt even when he was in the tea shop. And what was there at this left turn? Just a little warmth, nothing else. Actually, the wound had healed; it was the scab that remained and was itchy. He had not scratched it for many days now; today, he had turned left to scratch it.

A little further was that woman's house. She lived on the third floor. Yellow curtains hanging by a green window, and a withered plant in a pot just outside it. She kept her house spick and span usually. How had the plant in the pot withered? He stopped right at the staircase. He had no reason to go to her house. Still, he walked towards the house. Before his thoughts could compel him to turn back, he swiftly climbed the stairs and rang the bell. Her household help opened the door. Maybe she had been cooking; she held a ladle in her hand.

'Wait, let me ask Baby.'

Earlier, the household help would welcome him. Now he had to wait outside. The door stood half-open, and he was standing outside. He considered removing his shoes but wasn't sure what she would say. He began to grapple with his reasons. For a long time, neither the help was visible, nor did she come out herself. He stood leaning against the door which had opened further but was stuck on something. Maybe there was too much footwear kept behind the door.

Then, she came out.

She had stuck a pencil in her hair and was wearing a men's white shirt and a pair of red pyjamas. The shirt seemed like it had been worn hurriedly and improperly. She was wearing toe rings on her feet: two on one foot and only one on the other. She stood resting one foot on the other, her left hand behind her, maybe leaning against the wall.

He wanted to kiss her. He loved this casual manner, her improperness. Maybe this was his biggest reason for turning left.

'Why are you here?'

He had no reply to give. His list of reasons seemed childish in front of such carelessness. He remained quiet.

'Why have you come?'

'I wanted to have a cup of tea with you.'

Acting as if she didn't care, she answered, 'I don't want to . . .'

After a brief pause, she added, '. . . have tea with "you" . . .'

She had said precisely what she wanted to and was now quiet. Now it was his turn. He who had always wanted to avoid it. It was not as if he had just learnt how to avoid his turn. He had known how to avoid his responsibilities since childhood. In the game of hide-and-seek, he would never hide in a place where he was alone. He would often hide behind someone who was good at hiding. That way, the other person would get caught first and he wouldn't have to pay the price; he would be saved. He knew how to save himself and he had managed just fine until now. The games one plays during childhood are not merely games. Our participation in those games decides our role in life.

'If you have nothing to say, you may go.'

It was she who broke the silence.

'I did come to say something.'

But he had not come to say anything.

'Then speak up.'

After some more silence, not realizing what he was saying, he blurted, 'Whatever I am today was decided for me in my childhood. And I didn't particularly have any role in making that decision. I simply lived out, with honesty, what was decided for me.'

He let go of this sentence like he was releasing a burden. But this was not like conveying the news of a dear one's death after which one feels lighter. Maybe it was the lust that he was experiencing for this woman at that moment because of which he could say it.

'It is too late. You don't need to say all of this now.'

He had nothing more to say now. He tried to hold on to the edges of the conversation, but it felt so cold and impersonal that he began to feel very shallow trying to connect one end to the other. He could see that the woman didn't want to say anything. After having said what he had, at which he was surprised with himself, there was no scope to say anything else. He turned around and began to descend the stairs. When he reached the landing of the second floor, he heard the door being shut. That's when he experienced the pain for which he had climbed the three floors—the pain of parting forever. Now, the pain of not being able to save a relationship was overwhelming him swiftly.

He walked out of the building very quickly. Just before turning at the corner of the lane, he paused and looked back. She was not standing by her window. The yellow curtains were moving with the breeze. The dried pot looked very beautiful. He turned and left.

The pain was like the proof of being alive. It was an addiction that wove together the intricate illusion of being alive. However, nothing remains intact. In that weave, there is a web of loneliness that traps the small insects of pain. The web of loneliness acts like a cage for the insects of pain to live in.

He was terrified of spiders. Before entering his room, he would be extremely cautious about their presence. If he saw one, he would run to his sister shouting. She would then kill the spider with a broom. Only after she showed him the dead body of the spider would he re-enter his room.

This time, though, he didn't think about the spider. He took out a marker and wrote on the white fridge.

'What I am was decided for me in my childhood. And I didn't have any role in making that decision.'

* * *

'Enough . . . enough.'

She asked me to stop my story, and she got up. I remained seated where I was, near the temple. She began to wander alone in the tendu forest of Budhni. I could see her from where I was. The brown of her clothes was playing hide-and-seek amongst the trees. All the sunflowers seemed withered from that distance. I loved her so much that I wanted to leave her. I wanted to feel the flame of her love by staying away from her. Right now, everything was beyond my scope. She was beyond my scope. My love, just like the sunflowers—sometimes blooming and sometimes withered—appeared to be clinging to her. I wanted to plant all of them inside me, somewhere near my navel.

She returned after a while. Standing in front of me, she uttered the word 'return'.

She was standing in her balcony. The evening was the time for the cranes to return. The cranes had built a nest on the tree just in front. This was the time just before evening, prosaic.

She was aware that the tree in front would soon be full of white bulb-like cranes. This was her time. She celebrated this time all by herself; there was no scope for anyone else to join her. Right then, the doorbell rang and I stood before her with all my fatigue. She didn't invite me in, nor did she close the door. She turned away as if she didn't know me. Or perhaps knew me so well that it did not matter anymore.

Between us was a system in place. We had some unwritten rules that we had set at the beginning of our relationship. And because of those rules, we were alone in our personal spaces despite being in a relationship. This loneliness had created two islands and we both spent most of our time on our respective islands. The relationship could now be seen only from a distance.

She was standing in the balcony, on her island. I was right behind and wanted to swim to her island. This was absolutely against the rules we had made.

'Why don't you eat? There is food kept for you inside.'

She said this without looking at me. I returned to my island. All my swimming proved futile. I jumped into the water again.

'No, I am not hungry.'

Saying this, I, too, came and stood beside her in the balcony. No, this wasn't her island. I was far away from her. I felt as if swimming was taking me further away from her. She was peacefully counting the cranes. The tree was almost full of them. Right then, my gaze shifted to the road below and I could see myself standing there. I was standing on the road, looking at her standing in the balcony. I came back into the room immediately.

In a while, she came inside and she said a word as she came closer to me—'end'.

And I began to see the beginning of this story.

Tragedy

Diseased

In the face of an illness, all other problems in life seem frivolous. It was probably five in the morning. He was noiselessly going to the bathroom for the third time. His aunt was fast asleep in the next room. The rusted bolt of the bathroom didn't latch properly. One had to hang a towel outside to let others know that the bathroom was occupied. Inder had become urbane and was no longer used to going to the bathroom without latching it. This time, too, garnering all the remaining strength in his body, he bolted the door. And he vomited along with passing stool. After rinsing his mouth, he observed his face in the mirror. He had spent fifty years on this planet. Wrinkles, dark circles and fatigue. He rinsed his mouth again. The corners of the mirror had rusted completely. Amidst the rusted corners was a little space in the centre in which he observed his face. How did the rust even know its limit?

In the bathroom, the detergent bar and the bathing bar were kept together; one on top of the other. Some wet clothes were kept in a green bucket. He inhaled deeply and opened the latch, but the door didn't open; it was stuck. He used some more force, but it still didn't open. Because of his weak state, the moment he exerted himself he experienced a blackout. He called out to his aunt, but his voice didn't carry. He began to thump hard on the door. His body had become so weak that by calling out to his aunt and thumping on the door, his stomach began to grumble. He began to vomit. He threw up all the water he had drunk during the day. Only water.

Just then he heard his aunt from outside the door. 'Inder, Inder!'

His aunt pushed at the door, and with the second push it opened swiftly. The moment the door opened, Inder lost his balance, and his hand slipped into the small green bucket. Holding on to his aunt and the washbasin, he raised himself up. The moment he stood up he began to pant.

'What is the matter, Inder?' his aunt asked. Inder first looked at the mirror, and then at his aunt. She was extremely short. How could she manage to look into this rusted mirror? She would need to stand on something. What could she stand on? He suddenly began to search for that object in the bathroom.

'What happened, Inder? Has something fallen? Oh! Your whole body is burning.'

Just then he had a blackout, and he collapsed. His uncle had died of a cardiac arrest about six months earlier.

Inder had managed to visit from Mumbai for two days then. He had promised to return soon but wasn't able to. Office, work, relationship, preoccupation, laziness, boredom and the tiredness of living with one's own self . . . even all of these put together were not reason enough for not visiting. What could he tell his aunt? That he did not want to visit. He had not wanted to visit even now. He had simply wanted to keep chewing his cud somewhere. He was now used to living habitually. It didn't matter if thousands of people died somewhere or if a rat bit through a new shirt. Both these instances merely created a small bubble of pain and that bubble burst even before it became visible. His forehead would get creased, he would shut his eyes tightly once or twice, and then everything would become normal again, as if a film was playing. It seemed he knew all the scenes of this film; all the surprises were a mere act. Every instance had already been lived. Yet, he experienced hunger every day. And each day, the faint memory of the same taste made him go through the rituals of eating and sleeping.

When he opened his eyes, he was lying on the floor outside the bathroom. His aunt had put a cold press on his forehead. While lying on the floor he said, 'Aunty, let's go to the hospital.'

He began to almost crawl towards the hospital with his aunt. There was a private one just two lanes away. He would walk a little and then stop a while to catch his breath. His aunt would pour two mouthfuls of water down his throat as soon as he halted, and as soon as he gulped that water, his stomach would begin to churn again.

It was dawn. The market square was full of the hustle-bustle of newspaper sellers. Newspapers were being loaded on to bicycles. Breaking news and headlines were all scattered on the floor. The noise of *tann . . . tann . . . tann* took his gaze to the tea shop in the background. He loved having tea early in the morning. He forced his gaze away from the tea shop. A black street dog had been following him at a distance for some time now. Inder shooed him away a couple of times. The dog would stop when shooed away and then begin to follow him again. Since Inder was not walking fast, the dog, too, had to halt again and again. Whenever Inder halted and looked at the dog, it would also stop and start looking around for something, as if it was not following Inder. Getting irritated, Inder wished he could get hold of the dog and tell it that either it was with him or not. Tell me, tell me whether you are with me or not, Inder wanted to say to the dog. He lived alone in Mumbai. He had never wanted to live alone, yet he was alone. He wanted to get married and have a home of his own. This dream was complete with the image of having his morning tea with someone.

'Aunty, shoo away this dog.'

His aunt tried to make noises to shoo the dog away, but it was adamant.

'Never mind, it will go away on its own.'

In a while, Inder and his aunt were standing outside Shekhar Hospital. The name 'Shekhar Hospital' was painted on at many places on that building. In front was a huge iron mesh shutter, and inside, a dead silence. Only a tube light's glow was visible in the reception. Aunty made

Inder hold the water bottle and began to lift the shutter herself forcibly.

'Aunty, you won't be able to do it, let it be.' Defeated, they called out for someone. A man carrying a huge broom came out. He lifted the shutter up in one swift movement. The moment Inder entered the hospital, its typical smell of medicines, sweat, urine, the alive, the dead and the sick enveloped him. The time he had spent with his sister while she was in a coma, the last few years of his father battling Hepatitis-B and TB, the hassle of jaundice, the time when parents of several friends had been in hospital, donating blood, lifting dead bodies, post-mortems, the smell . . . smell . . . smell. . .

Inder was sprawled on a bench. The black dog looked at him from a corner, sitting just outside the shutter. His aunt came to him after completing all the paperwork.

'It is room number 104, first floor. The lift isn't working. Come, walk slowly.'

He began to climb the stairs slowly. His aunt had seemed lazy until yesterday, but now his illness appeared to have filled her with renewed energy.

She had found some work and a purpose. In her worry and concern, she wanted to help Inder climb the stairs. She would sometimes walk ahead of him, sometimes walk beside him holding his hand, and at other times, walk behind him. He gestured for her to go ahead. She became a little conscious and then walked towards room number 104. Struggling to walk, Inder reached the entrance of the room and caught his breath.

'Let the nurse change the bed sheet,' Aunty said. The nurse was changing the bed sheet, and pillow covers at her own pace. Inder looked at the room facing his—room number 103—the door of which was slightly ajar. Someone was lying on the bed, hands raised towards the sky. He looked at the hands carefully; they were a girl's hands, slim and delicate, and one wrist sported a watch. She was drawing something in the air with her fingers. He really wanted to see the face of that girl, but the door was only slightly open. He tilted a little to the left, but he could only see the girl's chin. Just then, the girl stopped drawing in the air. With a jerk, she lifted her head up and looked straight at Inder. He was startled, as if caught red-handed. 'I was caught red-handed.' This sentence began to ring in his head. He entered room number 104 and shut himself in the bathroom.

How strange it is to dream of being caught! Just before being caught, the nervousness, sweat and restlessness . . . and then he woke up. Aunty will get to know everything. The moment he woke up, he was relieved. Oh! It was a dream. But when he realized it was a dream, he wished to find out what happens immediately after getting caught. Inder quickly went back to sleep. Just like in a film, he tried to go back to his dream and begin it again from where he had left it the last time, but he couldn't.

Hospitals have a character of their own. Government hospitals are matter of fact. In their dirtiness, they are in your face. But private hospitals are adamant that they will not look like hospitals and this stubbornness is scary. Inder had surrendered. He had given his wallet to his aunt.

Whenever he opened his eyes, he saw her distributing money among people. After many bottles of IV and many trips to the bathroom, he came face-to-face with a doctor struggling with his English. He was surrounded by many of his assistants who were eager to please him. The doctor was a textbook image of a doctor—a thin black moustache, recently coloured hair, a slight paunch, loose pants held together with a belt, black shiny shoes and a nectar-like odour from his body.

'How are you feeling, sir?' the doctor asked, coming too close for Inder's comfort. Before Inder could reply, the doctor whispered something to his assistant and walked swiftly towards room number 103.

How substandard is everything that I have lived for so far, Inder thought to himself. In one moment, this sweet-smelling doctor could say that now it is very difficult; that everything shall wither away. And poor me will scatter, split and fall with a thud. Maybe there won't even be a noise. Right at that moment, I will be forcibly pushed into a cave running through the past where I lost Uncle. Maybe he will meet me there. Will I pretend to be busy even there? My cheap, lazy and rubbish acting.

He was suddenly reminded of his uncle's letters. Towards his last days, he had begun to write to him regularly. Some of his letters, Inder had half-read, some he hadn't even opened.

As soon as the doctor left, he fell asleep. He saw his uncle in his dream. He came to him carrying all his letters, and Inder kept saying, 'I am slightly busy right now.' But Uncle stood waiting. He would watch from his office window. Uncle would stand below the building waiting for him. From the keyhole of his apartment door, he could see Uncle spreading out the letters in the corridor. Inder woke up startled and stared at the wall in front of him. Did he want to go back to sleep and check whether he opened the door to his uncle or not? No, absolutely not. What had happened? What was the time? He saw that his aunt wasn't there on the adjacent smaller bed. There was no one in that small cave-like room. He began to experience some problem with his breathing. It felt as if this was the cave of his past, the room of his past, in which he had been forcibly stuffed. Then he saw the black dog sitting by the door watching him. He began to shout.

'Nurse, nurse! Sister, sister!'

An old woman, whose voice had the authority of a mother, came to check.

'What happened? You must rest. You will be administered many more drips.'

'No, that . . . that. . .'

The dog wasn't there.

'What happened?'

'Bathroom.'

That is all he could think of. The nurse made a face. She took out the IV tube from his hand, pushed it back into the bottle and put a small cap in place of the syringe.

'Go. Call out when you are done.'

'Yes.'

The nurse marched out. He didn't want to go to the bathroom. He simply wanted to come out of that dream. He wanted to run fast, very fast. He got up from the bed but lost his balance. His sweaty T-shirt clung to his back. He thought of turning on the fan. As he dragged himself towards the switch, his gaze drifted towards the door of room number 103. It was opened wider than the previous time. He felt his uncle's presence in there, waiting for Inder with all his letters. He took slow steps and reached the door of room number 103. He peeped inside and saw the girl. She was asleep. He looked around the room and saw that a lot of her clothes were strewn around. There was no one on the adjacent bed. A pair of small-sized slippers were lying on the floor. They looked as if they belonged to a child. He wanted to see her feet. Did these slippers really belong to those feet?

'Give me water.'

He was startled at the sound of her voice. She was looking straight at him with her big eyes; she had a straight nose, dishevelled hair and a wheatish complexion. Her age could not be deciphered from her face.

'The water is kept there.'

It was under the adjacent bed. He began to look for a glass. Unable to find one, he looked at her questioningly. It seemed as if she knew him and everything about him.

'There is no glass.'

Saying this, the girl extended her hand for the bottle. She sat up a little to drink the water. Inder saw her bulging breasts; she wasn't wearing a bra. As she drank water, she covered her chest with the sheet. Inder lowered his eyes. She must be twenty-eight or twenty-nine, he estimated. Then he began to curse himself. No, not exactly curse but the mindset just before cursing. He was fifty years old and yet could not control his desire to see a girl naked. He took the bottle from the girl's hands and as soon as he bent to keep it down, his body gave in. He felt dizzy, began to shiver and though he managed to wobble up to the other bed, he soon collapsed. He began to feel cold and started shivering. She was looking at him as he looked at himself. He didn't want to appear miserable. He somehow got a hold of himself and in the same posture picked up the water bottle and drank two sips. He was scared of his stomach complaining. The door of room number 103 was open. Inder looked towards his own room. He imagined himself still lying in room number 104. He was being administered the drip. He felt as if, while being in room 104, he was imagining himself to be in room number 103. Was he really here? He wanted to go to room number 104 and check on whether he was there or not.

'Don't go right now.'

'Yes.'

'No one comes here in the afternoons. I get bored. Please sit for some more time.'

'Yes, I will go after a while. I am not in a condition to go right now.'

He was here, in room number 103 and room number 104 was vacant. His office chair was also vacant. He was here. Room 104 appeared like a cave from this room. He began to make a comparative analysis of room numbers 103 and 104. This room had two windows, whereas his room had only one window. There was another window, but it had an air conditioner fitted on it, so it had been closed.

This room didn't have an air conditioner. He didn't need one. He needed light, he needed the sun. He didn't want to go into the cave. He was tired.

'I will be fine soon.' The girl said this to herself. 'What will you do after you get well? I mean, after leaving this hospital, what is the first thing you want to do?'

'I will eat golgappas. Look, down there, he sits beneath that tree every evening. There is a big crowd there every day. I will also go there.'

To see the golgappa seller's tree, he had to come close to her bed. He looked at the tree and smiled.

'And what will you do?'

'I shall take the first flight to Mumbai. Lots of pending work; I can only see my office desk and nothing else.'

Saying this he pressed the edges of the bed with both his hands. He felt the stretch in his shoulders. His neck just hung between both his shoulders. Why lie . . . why lie? The truth was that the moment he would be discharged from hospital, he would go straight to the girl he had been sleeping with nowadays. He had been physically intimate with her just once or twice. He felt a desperate urge to see her naked again. A burning sensation, a sharp burning sensation . . . where would she be right now? With whom? She must be standing very close to somebody with her beautiful body. Someone else would be touching her, caressing her, someone would . . . uff . . . this is insecurity. No, this is simply filth. The filth of defeat. Suddenly, he wanted to look outside the window to check whether the black dog was still waiting for him to come out of the hospital.

'What work do you do?' she asked after some silence. She was now sitting slightly upright. She had kept her pillow behind her head. Her sheet was covering her up only to her waist. He could see her breasts, but he couldn't take his eyes off her eyes. There was something in that girl's eyes. She knew him—everything about him—but was still making excuses and asking questions. This was just a dream, maybe. Only in a dream did one meet people who look like characters from a dream. And then one wants to surrender to those people.

'I help in selling stuff. I work in a company that makes advertisements for products so that you buy them. I have been in this field for many years now. Everyone says I am very good at it, but I feel I am not. I am not Inder; I myself am like a product which I try to sell every day using new methods. I have created an aura around me of sentences like "I am very different; I live a free life; and I am a nomad." I shine and polish this image of myself every day. Actually, I am a shirt that changes colour. I have simply washed and kept that shirt clean, made it shine, tried it in every season in the market. It always works. I always work. The most difficult task for me is living with myself, to live with my own self, to keep living continuously with all my falsehood. There is an emptiness around me for which I simply use others. They come and fill that emptiness for a while, but the moment they leave, I experience bitterness with my own self; from the fact that they were with me only briefly . . . each one of them. Then I move around again, looking for someone, finding someone. I actually want to make a confession. In some old church somewhere, there is likely to be an old priest who will say, "Go, God has forgiven you.'"

He became quiet, and she didn't say anything. Inder could not bear the silence. He could feel a drop of sweat crawling on his forehead. It had escaped his hair and was flowing down towards his eyebrow. He got up slowly. After walking two steps, he held on to the door of room number 103. He took a few deep breaths. And he heard the girl's voice.

'My name is Roshni.'

'I know you.'

'You know me?'

'Yes. If you hadn't told me your name, I would have called you Parul.'

'Why?'

Inder felt this was a dream from which he would wake up with the fear of getting caught. But right now, he was witnessing what happens after he is caught in the dream. What now? He did not reply to her 'why'. He began walking slowly towards room number 104, which seemed like a cave. He wanted to quickly disappear into that cave. He wished to go into a deep sleep, and he hoped that everything would have been erased when he woke up from the dream. His going into room number 103, his coming to this city, Uncle's death, his letters, Parul, his office desk, his name, everything ought to get erased. He was entering room number 104 as someone enters sleep.

Sleep is a delusion. Each time one gets to sleep soundly, it seems as if everything has been set right in an otherwise devastated life. As if an otherwise scattered household has suddenly been put back in order. And once everything is set right, one wouldn't allow anything to go wrong ever again. He was like dust in that disorderly household. He would sweep out that very same dust again and again, but it would accumulate and wait right at the doorstep . . . wait for the slightest opportunity to come right back into the house. He would work very hard professionally. He would remain busy, presuming there was an Inder in the future who would have an amazing life. In his imagined future, he would have bed tea with the love of his life. There was a swing in the balcony; there were dreams of sweet nothings for endless hours. Each time, the realization of these dreams would be just an arm's distance away, just like that black dog. It would walk along like a shadow but couldn't be caught; it couldn't be called one's own. At the beginning of each new relationship, he would also begin to dream of an imagined future. Part of it was also how the relationship would break. Who would go away this time? Who would leave whom this time? The Inder of his future seemed dismal to him. Sometimes, he felt the need to get his eyesight tested, but what would he say to the doctor—'Doctor saheb, please make me a pair of spectacles; my future looks bleak to me.'

He wished to buy a tabla. He wanted to learn to play it properly. Zakir Husain! *Tirkit dha . . . tirkit dha*!

'What happened?'

Aunty was cutting an apple sitting on the adjacent bed. 'What happened?'

'Oh, you were saying *tirkit, tirkit*!'

This wasn't a dream then; he was mumbling. An illness makes one so dependent.

'Nothing.'

He smiled. He was suddenly reminded of a day from his childhood when he was playing marbles on the porch and Aunt was chasing him around to feed him rajma-rice. She would make him have a bite every now and then. He would eat properly while playing, she felt. The veins in Aunt's hands were visible—raised, green veins. For the first time he realized how lonely she must be after Uncle had passed away. She had called him and said, 'Son, if you could come for a few days, it would feel good.' It was a small request, a plea. He could not make an excuse. He would have gone back by now had he not fallen ill.

'Aunty, come along with me to Mumbai. You can live with me there.' He said this softly, in a sick, teary voice.

Aunty offered him the apple slices.

'You are sick right now, that's why you are saying so.'

'No, Aunty, really—you must live with me.'

His aunt just smiled. He also became quiet. 'Have you brought my mobile?'

'Oh no! I couldn't find it. I was trying to find it, I called it too but could not hear any sound anywhere.'

'It's in the silent mode in the bag, in the inside pocket. Bring it when you go next.'

Just then an old nurse came and handed out a slip to his aunt.

'Bring these medicines.'

She said this and walked away.

'You have money?'

'Yes, yes. I will be back soon.'

'Aunty, I genuinely mean it. Come with me to Mumbai. We shall both live together there . . . go out for walks in the evening. The sea is close to my house. You like the sea a lot, don't you?'

Aunty continued looking at him.

'I really need you. I . . . I will feel good.'

'When you get better, I will also feel good.'

Your loved ones don't forget you quickly. And why should they? Things can't be set right without calculating the gains and losses of the past years. One doesn't always wake up to a dawn.

He saw that the door of room number 103 was shut. He felt as if the room had shifted away from his room. It had appeared close till the time he had not gone there. Now, room number 103 had distanced itself from room number 104. Just like all the other planets are furthering themselves from the earth; as if the earth is expanding. Just like his life was getting scattered while it was being lived. Relationships that were earlier at an arm's distance were now so far away that if he called out, all he would hear was his own voice echoing back. Does time push all relationships into a cave? Where there is only darkness? Our own mistakes . . . can they ever be amended? Just once . . . if everything could be set right just once. Could one ever get rid of the dust waiting at the threshold?

Both legs would shiver, my friend

He had just turned sixteen. He watched the Krishna Leela performance late into the night as he ate a wood apple. The moment he reached home, he started practising rotating a round plate on his index finger. He had grown fond of Krishna. The stories of Krishna and his *gopi*s, laced with lust, were now shared amongst friends. Then Krishna disappeared from the stories, and friends began to tell each other their imagined experiences of sex. He began to feel a stirring between his legs. This resulted in his deciding to learn how to play the flute.

The moment he thought about a flute, he was reminded of Ashutosh bhai. He used to go to his house for maths tuitions. He remembered seeing a harmonium kept in his room. Ashutosh bhai was an angry man. One day, when he sensed that Ashutosh bhai was in a better mood, he said to him, 'I want to learn music. Will you please guide me?' Ashutosh bhai immediately sat at his harmonium and began to hum something; it had no words to it. The maths tuition was abandoned; on top of that, his ears froze too.

One Sunday afternoon, Ashutosh bhai came home on a cycle. He called out, 'Bunty !' (His nickname was Bunty). He came out running and Bhai said, 'Come, I'll take you to meet my guru.' He wore his chappals and followed Ashutosh bhai on his Atlas Goldline. They reached the extreme end of the city, a Muslim neighbourhood. Ashutosh bhai stopped in a lane there. He put his cycle on its stand and locked it. Bunty also parked his cycle right behind his and locked it. Ashutosh bhai pointed out the house to Bunty. There was a board outside that had 'Music' written on it; alongside was drawn a veena. The board looked like it had been found in some archaeological dig. It had lost its colour from all sides. So much so that it had begun to look like a part of the wall. Inside, in a small room, Ashutosh bhai touched the feet of a big man. He also touched that old man's feet.

'Dadda, this is Bunty. He wants to learn the tabla.' Deceit! Krishna . . . gopis . . . suddenly, Bunty felt his legs weaken. He couldn't resist speaking and said, 'No, Dadda, I want to learn how to play the flute.' Ashutosh bhai stared at Bunty, who lowered his head. Ashutosh bhai came closer to Bunty and whispered in his ear, 'Are you making fun of Dadda?'

Bunty moved his head, indicating negative. 'Dadda has no teeth in his mouth; the air in his body is exhausted. How can he teach you to play the flute?'

In the end, Bunty purchased a tabla. *Dha . . . dhin . . . dhin . . . dha . . .* that was the beginning of his music. Dadda would teach a little and then sleep. Bunty would keep beating the tabla. Just then he saw the TV advertisement 'Wah Taj' featuring Ustad Zakir Hussain. He felt that Zakir Hussain was the Krishna of contemporary times, and the Krishna of today didn't play the flute; instead, he played the tabla. His Krishna fever vanished and instead of *dha . . . dhin . . . dhin . . . dha . . .* he jumped straight to *tirkit dha . . . tirkit dha.* Dadda would get annoyed at *tirkit dha.* 'What are these strange sounds that you produce? First learn to play simply.'

Parul would laugh a lot at this. Parul! It is all about Parul, really. She was an amazing singer. Even her laughter sounded like music. He would listen to her and quickly produce *tirkit dha . . . tirkit dha.* Parul would sing and he played along on the tabla. Parul would wear elegant salwar-kameezes. One day, Bunty was sitting with her to jam along when Dadda began coughing badly. Aai (Dadda's wife) had gone out to fetch vegetables. Parul went inside and brought some water. Bunty began to rub Dadda's back. Parul was bending to make Dadda sip water. Just then, he caught a glimpse of her breasts. He could suddenly hear the tender Raga Bhopali from somewhere. And he visualized Ustad Zakir Hussain. He became Krishna and started playing Raga Bhopali on the flute. Time stood still. His eyelids began to get heavier. He was forcing his eyes to remain open. He wanted to save this scene somewhere deep within, but his heart wanted a taste of it . . . wanted to consume it. Just then, Parul kept her hand on her kameez to cover herself. The flute lost all its music. Zakir Hussain vanished. He sat motionless at his spot. Nothing was the same after this incident. His gaze would keep caressing Parul's breasts all the time. He began to imagine going beyond that scene. Whenever his eyes would meet Parul's, he would be filled with longing. As if someone had punched him hard on his heart.

His heart had become a cycle's bell. Whenever he would think about Parul, the bell would ring. If someone called out to anyone, he would hear Parul's name. Every now and then, the bell would ring and his heart would sink. Now he didn't enjoy the tales of Krishna Leela. Krishna had many gopis around him. 'No, this isn't right,' he would say to his friends. Instead, he preferred the tales of Radha with Krishna. Whenever he would think about Parul—which was invariably followed by the heart ringing out its bell—he would feel a stirring sensation between his legs.

One day, after the music class, as soon as he mounted his Atlas Goldline to head for home, Parul called out.

'Bunty.'

'Aah!' This note . . . the music . . . he was stunned.

'Listen, let's go together. Where do you run off every day?'

'I . . . nowhere. Actually, I . . . ummm . . .'

If only his tongue were a tabla, he would have expressed everything with *tirkit dha* . . . *tirkit dha* . . . Right now, his tongue refused to say a word.

'Where do you live?'

'In the bazaar.'

'Where in the bazaar?'

'In the bazaar,' he answered like a simpleton.

'I am also going that way today. I have to go to the women's items shop.'

Both began to walk together. In a while, Bunty began to realize the problem with walking together and his legs began to shake for the first time. Everyone would notice him walking with a girl. He lived adjacent to the women's items shop. Choti, Raghu, Thontha, Bikki . . . all his friends' faces began to hover in front of him. The shivering in his legs increased. The cycle was between both of them. How could he refuse Parul? His house was located in the middle of the bazaar.

'My house is near the women's items shop . . . I mean, adjacent to it.'

'Oh, good! So, I can also see your house.'

Only the rich and affluent could afford to buy their children an Atlas Goldline Super Cycle. He had made his uncle buy him that cycle by pleading, arguing and fighting fiercely for it. He lived in a dilapidated house.

'You play the tabla very well.'

'Really?'

He wanted to keep the dialogue minimal. They had just entered the bazaar. He was walking at as much a distance as possible from Parul. He was holding his cycle in a strange and awkward manner. His shoulders were stiff, and his face had lost its colour. Almost everyone was staring at him. He hung his head low. Just as they were approaching the women's items shop, Choti, Raghu, Thontha and Bikki, and the most dangerous of them all, Goli, approached him. Goli was known in the locality as 'Goli the newspaper'. He knew all the news from the village and spread it with a few added details.

'Okay, then we shall meet tomorrow. My house is here.'

Bunty suddenly stopped. Parul had gone a bit ahead. Goli was observing them from the paan shop in front.

Bunty was standing in front of his house, but he pointed towards Mullaji's house, the one right in front of his house. Three-storeyed, Mullaji had it constructed recently. Parul walked towards the women's items shop, but didn't enter. She turned around to look at Bunty who was slyly looking at Goli. Bunty began to slowly walk towards Mullaji's house. He parked his cycle in front of it and waited. Parul was still standing outside the women's items shop. Goli stepped out of the paan shop. He took turns looking at Bunty and then Parul. Bunty began to climb the stairs of Mullaji's house. Right then, his aunt came out of his house and shouted, 'Bunty, where are you going, son? Come, I will serve you your meal.'

'Aunty . . . that . . . 100 . . .'

Bunty looked at Parul and then at Goli. His game was up. Mortified, he ran towards his house. His aunt could not understand anything.

'Oh, why have you parked your cycle there?' Aunt asked, but by then Bunty had rushed into the house. Goli began to laugh. Parul didn't go to the women's items shop. Instead, she began walking towards her house. Goli kept staring at her till the end of the lane.

Bunty wanted to avoid being outdoors. He chose to remain occupied in his inner dilemmas. He began to feel nobody understood him. He wanted to take Parul's name in every sentence, but he didn't have an answer for who Parul was. Neither did he go to the music class, nor did he meet his friends for many days. The image of Parul's breasts was imprinted on his mind. Whenever he would think about them, his legs would shiver. One afternoon, his aunt knocked at the door of his room. She said that some girl had come to meet him. Startled and confused, Bunty went straight into the bathroom. He quickly wet his hair, and then used the comb to flatten it. When he came out, Parul was sitting in the outside room on the sofa. Uncle was sitting beside her with an atlas. Uncle was in the habit of telling everyone how many countries he had lived in. Bunty sat near his uncle. Parul looked at him as if she had come to meet his uncle and not him. Uncle also included Bunty in his foreign trips. Bunty had been listening to these tales since childhood and so he got a little irritated.

His face still carried the shame of the lie of that day. Just then, Aunt came out and sent Uncle away for some task. In a while, she, too, went out saying that she had to see Varsha's mother. Bunty and Parul found themselves alone. It seemed that there was nothing they had to say to each other. Bunty smiled once or twice looking at Parul, but she remained composed. Then she finally said, 'Why haven't you come for the music class for so many days?'

'I will come tomorrow.'

Silence again.

'Your house is nice.'

And she became quiet. Bunty felt like crying over his mistake. He got up and went to his room. Parul remained seated outside for some time, and then called out to Bunty. At the third call, Bunty's teary voice responded, 'I am coming.'

Parul walked into his room. He was in the bathroom.

'Bunty, what is the matter?'

'Forgive me. I lied to you the other day about the house.'

'Forget it. Come out of the bathroom at least.'

'Please forgive me.'

'Okay, I forgive you. I thought perhaps you were unwell and so I came to enquire. Dadda was also worried that you had suddenly stopped coming for the class.'

He opened the door of the bathroom. When he came out, he was sweating profusely. Parul wiped his face with her dupatta.

'You are such a kid.'

Bunty found her breasts to be very close to him. His legs began to shiver and were unable to carry the weight of his body. He began to stumble. Parul held him and somehow managed to help him to the bed. As soon as he sat, he held both his knees with his hands, but his legs continued to shiver. Parul found this very strange. She touched his knees and the tickling sensation she felt made her laugh. She tried to stop Bunty's knees from shivering, using both her hands, but it didn't help. Her laughter put Bunty slightly at ease. He also began to laugh. Parul suddenly sat on the floor, and, with both her hands, she grabbed Bunty's knees tightly. The shivers slowed down. Parul's laughter stopped and she went and sat beside him. Bunty held her wrists with shivering hands, and she remained quiet. He slowly dragged his hands from her wrists to her face.

'What are you doing, Bunty?'

As soon as he heard that, the shivering of his knees stopped completely, and Bunty felt a sensation between his legs. Parul's hands were by her side.

'Bunty, this isn't right.'

A sudden fever crept over Bunty. He made Parul lie down on his bed and climbed on top of her. Parul closed her eyes. Bunty began to kiss her profusely. After a while, he was reminded of Parul's breasts. He removed her dupatta. But as soon as he did that, he didn't know what to do next. Parul began to get breathless and ill at ease. She was trying to use her hands to push Bunty away, but Bunty was in a state of passionate fervour. Suddenly, he realized that all the doors of the house were open. He got up to bolt the doors and saw Uncle coming back. It all ended there. Scared, he ran out of the room. He left Parul there in that state. Uncle was right in front of him; not knowing what to do, Bunty went straight into the kitchen while Uncle kept standing there. Parul came out of his room and went out of the house. Uncle stood stunned; he could not make sense of what had just happened.

After many days, one fine evening Uncle apologized to Bunty.

Bunty had, for the first time, seen another world; a world that lives outside of us and another that is alive within. His inner world was like a river. When you dive, you realize that, deep down, it is all green and beyond that greenery there is endless darkness. He was beginning to dive deeper and deeper. Inside, in that darkness, he could only see his own two eyes looking at him. He might have been scared, but he enjoyed the mystery. He might also have seen Parul's breasts, but now their vision didn't make his legs shiver. Facing Parul was similar to facing his eyes in the dark. He was scared for many days, which is why he didn't go to the music class.

One afternoon, as he stood in front of the music class, he could hear Parul singing inside. The beats! He remembered the beats he played on his tabla accompanying this raga. Someone else was playing those same beats. He went inside and saw Ashutosh bhai at the tabla. He sat in a corner. Parul merely glanced at him while singing, as if she didn't know him at all. Ashutosh bhai didn't even acknowledge his presence. Bunty felt as if no one liked his coming there. After the raga was over, Ashutosh bhai praised Parul. Dadda asked Bunty about his well-being. Parul was silent and in a while, she rose, touched Dadda's feet, and went out. Bunty also touched Dadda's feet and was about to exit.

'Listen, Bunty, you stay. I want to talk to you,' Ashutosh bhai said. Parul was waiting outside for him. He stood at the threshold looking at Parul; she understood. She smiled and went away alone. Bunty wanted to pick up the table, throw it at Ashutosh bhai's head, and go with Parul. But, no, good boys don't do this; they are scared, and they are cowards. He was also in the queue to becoming a good boy. His entire childhood had been spent in that struggle. Like a good boy, he stayed on this side of the threshold; he never crossed it. Ashutosh bhai touched Dadda's feet and gestured at Bunty to come along with him. Bunty, obeying his instructions, followed him.

They talked in the lane.

'So how is the music going?' asked Ashutosh bhai.

'Okay . . . fine . . . good,' he answered, stammering. 'Parul is a good girl.'

'What!'

'Why, don't you like her?'

'Yes! I mean . . . she sings well.'

'Okay, so you like her singing?'

'She sings all right, Ashutosh bhai.'

'Why, do you play better?'

'What!'

'You play with her when she sings, don't you! Dadda was saying you think you are Zakir Hussain.'

'I? No, bhai.'

'Do you know about Parul's father? He is a doctor. They have pedigree dogs. Parul even speaks to her dogs in English. Do you know how to say anything in English except "My name is Bunty"?'

Bunty knew where this conversation was headed. He began to look at the third button of his shirt and became quiet. He was now repenting. How he wished he had actually thrown the tabla at Ashutosh bhai's head! He wouldn't be facing all these questions now.

'Why are you quiet now? Answer me. How much English do you know? If you have to take Parul's dogs for a walk, just "My name is Bunty" won't be enough. What? Do you want to take her dogs for a walk?'

'Why would I take her dogs for a walk, bhai?'

'Okay, so you want to take her for a walk? What! Are you even listening to what I am saying?'

Ashutosh bhai's voice was full of anger. Bunty's chin was quivering, and his eyes were watery.

'You are doing all this in front of that almost-blind old man! What! What is your age? You had set out to learn the tabla but got to learn something entirely different instead. What to do!'

At this, Bunty could no longer hold back his tears. He began to cry bitterly. Ashutosh bhai was now quiet. He dropped Bunty home. When he reached

Bunty's home, he caressed his head and said, 'That, in front, is Mullaji's house. This is your house, you know, Bunty? Tomorrow onwards take the morning class and concentrate on learning the tabla.'

Like a good boy, Bunty listened to Ashutosh bhai quietly till he went to the paan shop and met with Goli. After a while, he bent his head and entered the house. He felt as if he was the worst sinner in this entire village. He wanted to repent for his sin. He spoke to his uncle about repentance. Uncle asked him to go to the Kale Mahadev temple and seek forgiveness with a pure heart; he would surely be forgiven. Following what his uncle had told him, he would go and sit at the temple every afternoon. He would repent for hours but every now and then he would envision Parúl's breasts. He would beat his head and then again apologize to Kale Mahadev for it. How big a sinner am I, he would say to himself! He felt that there was no respite from this sin. He had to do something. Anything. He was not eating properly. He had developed dark circles. He went to the music class every morning. Whatever Dadda said he accepted with his eyes lowered. He neither wanted to become Zakir Hussain nor Krishna. He wanted to simply disappear, be invisible. In bouts of extreme anger, he would imagine breaking tablas on Ashutosh bhai's head but this, too, would fill him with a deeper sense of sin. He would again go and sit at the Kale Mahadev temple for repentance.

One morning, as he was beating the tabla in a disinterested manner, he saw Parul at the door. He felt a pang, as if someone had driven a nail into his heart. Bunty's face twisted. Parul didn't sit in front of him but by his side. Dadda was happy to see her. He forgot about Kale Mahadev and all his days of repentance. Whatever had happened that day in his room between him and Parul had become their secret. But even the secret was full of mystery for both of them. The secret was pulling them towards each other like a string. Bunty didn't have the courage to look at Parul, but he could breathe again. He regained his appetite. He felt as if he had not eaten for many days. Parul

began to sing, and he began his *tirkit dha . . . tirkit dha . . .*
on the tabla; he became Zakir Hussain again.

After finishing with the music class, both of them
walked up to the end of the lane without uttering a single
word. Bunty turned left and Parul right. Bunty let out a
deep breath as soon as he turned left, as if he had been
holding his breath until now. Suddenly, he heard Parul
call out.

'Bunty, I have some work at the women's items shop.
Can I come with you?'

Bunty wanted to say 'no' but his head nodded a 'yes'.
Parul started walking with him. This time, Bunty wasn't
scared. He didn't think of any of his friends. He was
smiling. Meanwhile, Parul took out a peacock feather from
her music book and gave it to him.

'I had brought this for you the day after, but you
stopped coming to class. So . . .'

'It is very beautiful.'

Bunty interrupted her and kept staring at the feather.

'One more thing.'

She took out a small diary from her bag. 'This is also
for you.' Bunty saw there was something written on the
first page of that diary. He didn't have the courage to read
it. He hurriedly kept it in his pocket.

'There is one more thing.'

She took out a pen from her bag.

'Enough. I can't take so many things.'

'Keep them; they are for you.'

Bunty kept the pen as well. It had the name of some
pharmaceutical company printed on it. That's when he

was reminded that Parul's father was a doctor. He was also reminded of what Ashutosh bhai had told him.

'You know I don't know English?'

'What?'

'And I am not too fond of dogs either?'

Parul didn't understand what he was saying. Bunty had made his confessions and so he felt lighter. He began laughing. Parul, too, laughed with him.

At the women's items shop, Parul spent a while asking about the cost of various bangles. Then she bought a strip of bindis and left. Bunty was standing at his door after changing into new clothes. Parul smiled when she noticed this.

Bunty opened the pocket diary. He felt a strange fear as soon as he opened it. He went and shut the door to his room. He turned the first page, on which was written: 'For the tabla-player, Bunty'. Below it was a smiley. In one corner of the page, she had scribbled her own name: Parul. Bunty kept staring all night at the peacock feather kept by his pillow.

As if someone had stirred sugar into his days, everything was now sweet for Bunty; every presence complete.

The following morning, he was sitting in front of Parul. Parul noticed that Bunty had placed the pen she had given him in his shirt pocket. Dadda was teaching him a new beat, but his entire focus was on Parul. Just then, Ashutosh bhai appeared at the door.

Sometimes, dreams are brutally shattered. The echo of that shattering sound keeps ringing in one's ears for several years.

Ashutosh bhai kept waiting for Parul to leave. Parul got up when it was time, touched Dadda's feet, and went away. Bunty didn't even have the courage to stir. In a while, Ashutosh bhai got up. He, too, touched Dadda's feet and went out. Bunty remained seated where he was. Ashutosh bhai was staring at him while unlocking his cycle.

'Come on! Are you going to sit there alone and sing a bhajan?'

Bunty forgot to touch Dadda's feet and came out. 'The weather is fine in the morning.' Ashutosh bhai initiated a conversation.

'Yes.'

'What do you want to do in life?'

'What, bhai?'

'What happened?'

'I want . . . tabla . . . And I want . . . want . . . want . . .'

'I met with your aunt just before coming here. You belong to a good family.'

'What did you tell Aunty?'

'I haven't said anything yet. What has happened to your face?'

Bunty touched his face.

'It's pimples, bhai.'

'You are becoming hot-blooded.'

'What!'

'You and I are learning music from the same guru. So, what does that make us?'

Bunty didn't understand.

'So we are like brothers. By the same logic, what does Parul become to you?'

Bunty became quiet. Ashutosh stopped on the way. 'What does Parul become to you then?'

'Sister, I guess, bhai.'

'Sister. She is your sister. Say it again.'

'She is my sister.'

Bunty's eyes welled up with tears. This time, along with the tabla, he also wanted to break the harmonium on Ashutosh bhai's head.

'I am sorry, Ashutosh bhai. Parul is my sister.' This placated Ashutosh bhai. The matter was now out of Kale Mahadev's jurisprudence. Bunty felt he was not even good enough to apologize. All this led him to renounce music at the earliest and, according to the trend of those times, he bought sulphas tablets from the market. For many nights, he slept with the tablets under his pillow. In moments of deep sadness, he would look at them and then put them away.

One evening, Uncle came to his room. Bunty was lying on his bed. Uncle put his hand on his shoulder. Bunty woke up, startled.

'I am going to stroll down the ghat; I'm not feeling too well. Will you come along?'

Bunty accompanied him without saying anything. They both went and sat at the riverbank. It was time for the evening prayer ceremony. They could hear the chanting of the prayer and the ringing of the bells from the temple close by. Bunty felt very calm.

Uncle was very fond of laddoos from Raju's sweet shop. Bunty had bought some on their way there, and Uncle had already eaten his share. Bunty's share was lying untouched; he had barely tasted them.

'Oh, Bunty, I met Parul in the bazaar. Perhaps she didn't recognize me.' As soon as Uncle mentioned Parul's name, Bunty began to cry loudly. He was so embarrassed that he walked up to the river and began to splash water on his face. Uncle kept sitting where he was. He picked up Bunty's share of laddoos and kept them with him. Bunty returned in a while. For a long time, neither Uncle nor Bunty said anything.

Uncle could not bear the awkwardness and so he began to eat the laddoos.

Finally, Bunty said, 'I am very upset, Uncle.'

'What's the matter?'

'Forget it . . .'

'You are at a terrible age. It makes you want to do the impossible . . . everything . . . from love to revolution. At your age, it feels as if everything is in your control. It seems that whenever you open your fist, you will find everything you ever wanted lying there for you. And what's interesting is that you will even get what you want; but, everything comes at a price. You have to pay that price. There is no escape route. I am telling you the truth: life is very long. You have a lot of time; don't open your fist so early.'

For the first time, Bunty understood what someone had told him.

'Until when can I keep conversing with my closed fist?'

'Fists are not for dialogues; they are the reasons why we manage to live through all our difficulties.'

'Sometimes I feel I should end it all.'

'That is very easy. Anyone can do that. You have plenty of time on your hands. That is what the problem is. Once you get started on your path in life, you will have no time to even think about all these things.'

'So will I forget Parul?'

'You will forget all of this, but you will never be able to forget Parul. This longing will turn into a gentle tug at your heart, but a longing nevertheless.'

Bunty felt as if Uncle had breached into his inner world to tell him all this. After this incident, he felt closer to Uncle. Music, Krishna, Zakir Hussain . . . he had left everything behind, but he remembered Parul. The longing—the pen she had given him, the peacock feather, the diary—he had kept it all safely and carefully with him.

One day, Parul came to Bunty's house on the pretext of going to the women's items shop. Aunty had gone to meet Varsha's mother, and Uncle was alone in the house. He called her inside.

'Is Bunty home?'

'No, child, he isn't here.' He offered her a glass of water.

'He stopped coming to the music class, so I thought . . .'

Her sentence broke halfway.

'He has gone to the city. We got him admitted into a boarding school. He is going to live there from now onwards.'

Parul didn't drink the water; she turned around to look at Bunty's room. Uncle said, 'I will get you a cup of tea.' By the time he brought the tea and biscuits, she had already left. Uncle wrote letters to Bunty at times. He wrote about his own things and enquired about his well-being; but he never ever mentioned Parul's visit to him.

Roshni

When he opened his eyes, he saw Roshni sitting beside him . . . the girl from room number 103. He couldn't believe it. He ran his hand through his dishevelled hair, straightened his pillow and sat up.

'I have come to see my fellow patient.'

'Sorry, I was asleep. Have you been sitting here for long?'

'It felt good watching you sleep. What did you dream of?'

'I . . . don't know.'

'Say it without thinking too much. I was observing your face. Every now and then, there were creases on your forehead. Tell me quickly.'

'I . . . don't know. It was some juvenile stuff—my uncle, home and a lot more. I don't dream often; this must be a side effect of all the medicines.'

'Tell me exactly what you saw in the dream . . .'

'I saw that I was sitting with my uncle at the riverbank. We were eating laddoos and he was asking me about his letters. His letters . . . that's all I can remember. Nothing else.'

How easy it was for everything to get mixed up. What he saw and what he had lived! He had forgotten the art of speaking the truth. He was now accustomed to saying everything in a presentable format. He was so used to this that he could never state the plain, simple truth.

'Should I tell you about my dreams?'

Roshni was reminded of many of her own dreams. 'Do you see many dreams at once?'

'No, I have been here for many days and I remember all my dreams. All of them.'

'Okay, wait for two minutes. Let me use the bathroom first.'

The nurse was summoned. The IV drip was removed, and he went to the bathroom. All the while, Roshni calmly remained seated. She kept beating at the stool's leg with her own left leg, like a slow beat of some music. In a while, he came out . . . face washed, hair neatly slicked back. The nurse was called, and the drip was administered again. As soon as the nurse left, both Inder and Roshni went back to paying attention to each other. All the time the nurse had been around, they had pretended they didn't know each other.

'Tell me,' Inder said.

'First, I will tell you about the dream I had last night. Someone was making me fly. I was walking into the dark night, but my walking was like flying. I wasn't flying on my own; someone was making me fly. I was on a lane and as soon as I reached the turning, the sea lay sprawled before me. And morning dawned. In the distance, someone was standing in the waters. I turned and looked back, and it was still night behind me. I began to walk towards that man; the waves of the sea were touching his feet. He had a thread in his hand that he was pulling at.

'And there was a big pile of thread near his feet. It seemed like he had caught some fish. He began to pull at that thread more vigorously. I now began to run towards him. As I approached him, his thread broke. He turned around and looked at me. It was you.'

'Me?'

'Yes.'

'It is strange that I was in your dream.'

'You appeared in my dream one more time. I saw you were going into some old house that was pulling you towards it. There was someone else's name written outside the house. You sensed that a lot of people were asking you not to enter that house, yet, there was no one around you. The moment you opened the door to that house, you got lost. When you turned around, that door had vanished. I saw you roaming around like a lost soul.'

'And?'

'I thought I should tell you about these two dreams about you.'

'Perhaps the medication had affected me too strongly the other day. I was led astray. You must have been surprised by my strange behaviour. Maybe that is the reason you saw such weird dreams.'

'I keep dreams away from my personal life. I don't interpret them in the context of my personal life.'

'When I was lost in that house, where were you?' 'I was asleep.'

She began to laugh aloud at this. Inder, too, began to laugh.

'I don't know . . . I was dreaming that dream; I wasn't a part of it.'

'How long have you been here?'

'I told you I have been here for a long time now. I don't exactly remember for how long.'

'What do you do?'

'I live here in a hostel. My family doesn't know that I have been hospitalized; they will create a scene. I had jaundice. It was cured by an apothecary's magic tricks but when it resurfaced, it required me to be admitted in hospital. I am a lot better now. A few more days . . .'

'And then golgappas . . .?'

'I don't know.'

'I don't know? Didn't you say that the first thing you would do after being released from here is eat golgappas?'

'That's what I wanted to do then; now I don't. Now I want to go straight to my hostel room. I miss it. I have a cat named Winter. I don't know how she is managing. I like cats. They don't easily acknowledge someone as their own and even if they do, they don't bother much. They don't let anyone become their master.'

'I don't like any animals.'

'And humans?'

'What kind of a question is that?'

'It's a straightforward question.'

'I don't know. I mean . . . I like them, and sometimes, I don't. No, maybe after a while I can't tolerate anyone.'

'And yourself?'

'Why are you asking me these questions? How much do you know me and what right do you have to . . .'

Inder became quiet. He turned his pillow and lay down. Roshni felt awkward. She got up to leave.

'I must go.'

'Stop! Sorry. Do sit for a while. Aunty must be about to come back; you must meet her, too. She feels I am stuck here and worries a lot unnecessarily.'

'You do seem stuck; that's why I, too, came here.'

'To pity me?'

'I don't know how to show pity.'

'Okay. Do sit down, at least.'

Roshni began to smile. Inder sat up again. 'Should I tell you what I actually came to say?'

'Do tell.'

'I was in a very bad shape till about twelve days ago. I felt my body was giving away gradually. Then something happened. I haven't spoken about this to anyone. It seemed as if from that point onwards, I began to get better. Really, I did. Meanwhile, I also began to feel that I have grown up. I know the other Roshni who had walked into this hospital. It felt as if she was a good friend of mine; but she wasn't me.

I have grown up now. When you suddenly left my room that day, I couldn't help thinking about you. I even made up a story about you.'

'What story?'

'Forget it; it's childish.'

'I want to hear it.'

'It was just for me. I have partly forgotten it. Okay, I should go now. Gagan is about to come by.'

'Who is Gagan?'

'He is a friend; he takes care of me.'

'Who else comes to see you?'

'I have many friends. Initially, a lot of them used to come over. They assumed I wouldn't make it. Now that I am beginning to get better, it's only Gagan who comes to meet me. Other than him, my maternal uncle comes

by, too. I don't like him at all. He has promised that he
won't mention my hospitalization to anyone at home. Had
you been admitted in a hospital in Mumbai, would a lot of
people have visited you?'

'Yes, I should hope so. But I am not sure.'

'Why? Are you . . . I mean . . . ?'

'I am single. I only have my aunt; no other relatives.
And a few friends with whom I remain busy.'

In a few words, Inder had spoken the whole truth. He
wanted to talk about Parul, too . . . everything . . . but he
remained quiet. Roshni walked away to her room in silence.

She shut the door the moment she reached her room.

Her father had died when she was twelve. He was
survived by his wife, Roshni and her younger sister. She had
seen the smiling face of her father in her sleep. Thereafter,
he never returned home. She carried with her the image of
that face even today. Soon after her father's death, Roshni
felt an emptiness in the house—a vacuum created by her
father's absence. This actually saddened her more than
her father's demise. She felt as if her mother's eyes were
constantly searching for something. She decided that she
would fill that space; someone had to. Roshni began to
behave exactly like her father. She began to wear trousers
with shirts. She would get her younger sister dressed for
school, make her lunch, and kiss her goodbye before putting
her on the tonga to school. Roshni accompanied her mother
to the market and even kept household accounts. One day,
she scolded her mother just as her father did when the food
was not cooked well. Her mother was in shock and looked
at her daughter with unbelieving eyes. Roshni felt as if she

had been caught out. Her role play was no longer that; she had actually begun to live it. It was about to come to an end.

After this incident, Roshni was not as firm in her father's role as she had been earlier. But whenever she found the space, she would become her father. Her father's cigarette butt would be kept hidden in her school bag. When alone in her room, she would take it out and hold it in her fingers. She felt that her voice had begun to get deeper. She would speak in a baritone to her father's picture, telling him all her secrets. She would swear to take good care of the house. The picture was kept hidden under her pillow. Her mother, who always remained quiet, and her sister, who was too young, were oblivious to the changes happening to her.

Sinha Uncle's visits to their home became more frequent. Initially, Roshni really liked it; Sinha Uncle was one her father's old friends. He had said so himself, though Roshni didn't remember ever seeing him with Papa. He was fine, but something wasn't quite right, especially his behaviour with Mother, because it had a strange farce-like quality to it. Roshni didn't like it although Mother would be happy when he came over. Roshni was never able to express her displeasure to anyone. Sinha Uncle would always get a chocolate for her younger sister and while giving it, he would forcibly pinch her cheeks. Mother would sometimes go out with him and return late at night. One night, she talked to her mother about her displeasure. There was a lot of bitterness inside her that she couldn't hide. Mother said, 'Speak properly about him; he is just like your father.'

After this incident with her mother, Roshni's role-play seemed a sham to her. Late at night, she would take out her father's picture from under her pillow but wasn't able to say anything. She would simply cry. She was old enough to make sense of the relationship between her mother and Sinha, who wasn't like her father at all. He would laugh in a very crude way. His hands were rough, and his sweat could be smelt from a distance. He would eat with his mouth open, and his stomach was the largest part of his body. He would often make her sit on his lap in a way that his beard would poke her. The biggest difference between him and Papa was that Sinha didn't smoke cigarettes.

One morning, he came in his jeep and took everyone to a hill station for two days. He had made all the arrangements with a lot of theatrics. After a day-long journey, when they reached the hotel, she and her sister were put up in one room and her mother and Sinha were in another.

Roshni removed her father's picture from under her pillow and hung it on the wall of her room. Sinha and her mother got married. Mother told Roshni and her sister that he was to be addressed as Papa from now on. She wanted to tell her mother that it was she who was the father in this house. She had decided to become Papa after he went away; that she was trying to become Papa.

The house was longer home for Roshni. Sinha Uncle was a changed man as soon as he became Papa. His behaviour made it difficult for everyone to live with him. Whenever he found Roshni alone in the house, he would call her towards him on some pretext and then try to get intimate. Roshni was scared of this odd behaviour of her new father. She tried talking to her mother, but she had accepted her new husband completely. Sentences like 'He will change for the better' kept up the pretence. Sometimes she would manage to escape from her new father; sometimes not. Roshni wanted to leave that house. That's when she met Gagan who was her new father's friend's son. In between visits to their house, he grew fond of Roshni. Realizing that she was fond of reading, Gagan would bring her books. One day she was reading the anthology of writer Gyanranjan titled *Journey*. On the forty-second page of that book, Gagan had scribbled something in extremely small letters. While returning the book, she added a few words of her own to it. This is how the sequence of the forty-second page began, bringing Gagan and Roshni closer. Roshni expressed her wish to leave the house. Even though the relationship existed merely on pages, it was a written one. Gagan's fondness for reading meant he was deeply attached to everything written. He arranged a job for himself in the city and Roshni followed him in a few months on the pretext of higher studies. While leaving her house, she felt as if she was leaving it forever. While embracing her mother, she had softly said, 'Forgive me.' Mother seemed not to have heard this. Her younger sister was happy; she knew Roshni would call her to the city soon, which Roshni didn't. She carried with her an old photograph of the four of them as a happy family.

Gagan was still just a friend. The relationship of the forty-second page still continued. Roshni was now living in a hostel. Gagan was completely engrossed in his work.

She was lying down in her hospital room and her hands were searching for something in the air. Then she began drawing a picture in the air with her fingertip. With a loud thud, the door to her room opened. Gagan was standing in front of her. He looked very handsome in a blue shirt. He had also shaved that day. Roshni asked him to come closer to her. As Gagan came and sat on her bed, Roshni pulled him closer and kissed him. While he would always close his eyes, Roshni liked to keep hers open. She liked to watch herself kissing Gagan, who seemed to be trying to locate the feeling of a mild ache somewhere in his body.

'You are smiling again,' Gagan said, while slowly moving away, and Roshni laughed.

'Sorry . . . sorry.'

'I knew you would laugh at me!'

'I said I was sorry. You know you look very cute.'

'I am not cute!'

'You are also looking very handsome today!'

'Thanks. You always find me handsome in clothes that you have gifted me.'

'Oh! What is the matter? Why are you so irritated?'

Gagan fell silent. They were friends and, at times, they crossed the line; Roshni was the one who decided when. Gagan would get annoyed about this. When they would get into an argument over this, Roshni would make it clear that she did not want to lose him as a friend and so she loved him within limits. Since Gagan had read Roshni's words in her books, and he was always loyal to the written word, he agreed with whatever she said.

'There is a man in the room in front. He came to visit me; his name is Inder. He suddenly walked into my room. He was sick and was stumbling, and yet spoke such strange things. Then I went and visited him in his room. I told him about my dreams and the dreams that I want to dream.'

During Gagan's silence, Roshni changed the topic. Gagan had brought along some eatables; he was busy taking them out. He was pretending not to listen to what she was saying. 'I don't know why I get attracted to people of this age despite the fact that I want to seek revenge from them. But when I get close to them, I want them to hit me, scold me, insult me . . .'

Gagan stopped what he was doing and turned his full attention towards Roshni. 'Who is he?'

'Someone who is going through a mid life crisis. Well, maybe not a crisis. Perhaps he is alone . . . lost . . . I don't know.'

'What did he say?'

'Though he wanted to speak the truth, he only managed a garbled story.'

Gagan didn't want to know any more.

'You will be discharged tomorrow.'

'What?'

'Yes, I just saw your reports at the reception. The only issue now is weakness, and I have been told to take care of your diet.'

'That is good; I can live with you for a few days.' 'No, you go and stay at your hostel; I will keep visiting you.'

'Oh! Someone is living with you.'

'Yes. Dipti comes home. As it is, she has a lot of issues with you.'

'She isn't wrong. Shouldn't she have issues with me?'

'No, she should have issues with the girl who used to write on the forty-second page; not you.'

'But I am that girl.'

'Trust me, you are not her.'

Gagan was being honest and upfront. He put something back in the bag and was about to leave.

'Will your uncle come tomorrow morning?'

'No, he is out of town.'

'Okay, then I will come to take you to your hostel. Be ready by nine.'

'Where are you going?'

'Dipti is waiting downstairs.'

Roshni liked Gagan a lot. He was soft-spoken and had a wheatish complexion. She also liked his lips a lot. Whenever someone else entered his life, she would feel a strong attraction towards him. So much so that she almost waited for another girl to come into his life. He had become very serious regarding Dipti, but Roshni wasn't able to stop herself. Today, she didn't want to kiss Gagan, but she had smelt Dipti. Another girl's fragrance on Gagan's body was very arousing for her.

She kept waiting for Gagan until late into the night, but he didn't come. Suddenly, she began to think about the night her new father had entered her bed. She had pretended to be asleep. He came and held her. If she wanted to, she could have shouted and put an end to everything. But she remained quiet. That's when she began to enjoy this torture. She wanted him to treat her badly . . . to claw her, hit her . . . she started to cry, but these were not tears of fear. It was a weird experience. She was scared because she was finding a strange kind of solace in this. Roshni had left her home fearing that very solace.

She got up from her bed and began pacing up and down in her room. Something wasn't quite right.

In a while, she found herself in Inder's room. She didn't know what it was; on the one hand she wanted to take revenge on someone and on the other hand, she wanted to be defeated. She touched Inder's feet gently. Inder opened his eyes and sat up with a start.

'What happened? Is everything all right?'

She didn't answer him. She sat next to him and removed the drip from his hand. Keeping her hand on his chest, she gently pushed him. Inder was looking into her eyes as he lay down. Roshni removed her slippers and, spreading out Inder's left hand, she rested her head on it and lay next to him.

'You know what you are doing?' Inder asked hesitantly. Roshni placed her index finger on his lips. She turned her face towards him and was now clinging to him.

'Are you visiting me in my dream?' Inder asked after a few moments of silence.

'You dream too much nowadays because of the medicines.'

'Who is dreaming this dream?'

'This isn't a dream.'

'Can I touch you? Are you here?'

Roshni was quiet.

'I can't do anything.'

'That's what you feel, but you can do it.'

'Will we remember this in the morning?'

'Why are you thinking about the morning?'

'I want to live in this moment.'

'You are living.'

'I am not living; I can't see this happening. Can I switch on the light?'

'No, I am sleepy.'

'I don't want to sleep.'

'I haven't come here to sleep.'

'Will you go away in the morning?'

'I don't know.'

'Can all this not come to a standstill? Here . . . just like it is.'

'No.'

'Why?'

'If you want to stop this, then I will have to go.'

'This will end.'

'This is ending.'

'I am about to cough but I don't want to. I am scared that it might awaken me out of my dream.'

'You can cough and check.'

'No, I can't take that risk.'

Inder turned towards Roshni. Her head was resting against his warm chest. They were both breathing harder. Inder was watching everything, smelling everything, feeling everything . . . He shut his eyes tight and then opened them, not knowing whether he was asleep or awake. He gently touched Roshni's eyes and then her lips. Roshni opened her mouth. As Inder put his finger in her mouth, she bit it.

'Aah!'

'See, it isn't a dream,' Roshni murmured.

They started kissing each other. In a while, Roshni's eyes began to well up, and between his deep breaths, Inder called her 'Parul'.

Scan QR code to access the
Penguin Random House India website